MAGNOLIA 2

MISS JAZZIE

Magnolia 2

Published in the United States of America.

Published by Cole Hart Signature, LLC.

Mailing List

To stay up to date on new releases, plus get information on contests, sneak peeks, and more,

Go To The Website Below...

www.colehartsignature.com

MAGNOLIA

The sirens almost blinded me as I got closer to the scene. Earlier, I heard the shots of cowboys and Indians, and I ran to hide under my bed. That was a norm for me, but I knew what to do not to get hit by a stray bullet. Whoever was shooting was hitting with a machine gun because the bullets wouldn't stop. Automatic, probably hitting the target with every round.

Just then, I thought about my mother and father leaving the house earlier to get dinner because Moms didn't feel like cooking. I was cool with that because I wanted Chinese food from the spot called Chinese Kitchen. My mouth watered at the thought of the boneless chicken and combination rice that I knew they would bring back. I knew they would take a while, but I waited because my mother said they had to handle "adult business," and I knew not to question it. I wasn't trying to have my lips snatched from my face.

I grabbed Jahari as we waited under the bed for the bullets to stop. I had to protect my brother because I knew he was scared. Although he somewhat grew up with the shit, he would never get used to it. His body lay next to me, shaking like a leaf, but he was quiet. The only sound was his breathing because it was heavy. We waited until the shooting stopped completely before climbing from under the bed. We took slow but steady steps to the front door and went out.

We looked to the left and heard the blaring sirens and saw the flashing red and blue lights. The entire street was lined up with people trying to see what was going on. People on top of people were walking, trying to get as close as they could get to see the action.

I grabbed my brother's hand and walked toward everybody else. For some reason, I felt like it was just me and my brother walking alone. Everybody around us disappeared. Our steps got slower the closer we made it to the yellow caution tape. We got close enough for the tape to touch us before we were stopped.

"Hey, you can't come behind here," one of the officers said, and I looked at him.

I tried to get a better look at the scene before us because I wanted to know what was going on. I held tight to Jahari's hand and squinted to get a better look. The officer tried to shield my eyes from the scene, but it was too late. I had already seen it. I burst through the tape, taking him with me as I made my way through the crowd, making sure to hold my brother's hand tight. As we got closer, I noticed my father's Chevy Caprice. I knew it was his because he was the only nigga in the hood with one. My mother's name was spray painted on the driver's side door, and he had custom 28-inch rims with his initial in the center. I pulled my brother behind me because I didn't know what we were about to walk up on.

"Hey, kids. Don't get too close." Another officer came over, but it was a black female. She looked familiar, but I couldn't place her face. I was determined to see what was going on.

"Let them go," I heard someone say from behind us, and she unhanded me.

We walked closer, making our way slower through the sea of officers. I had to make sure my brother was shielded from whatever we were about to see. I peeked forward, and tears rimmed my eyes.

Instantly, they started to fall down my cheeks. I tried to wipe them so Jahari wouldn't see. One of the neighbors grabbed him as I walked closer. My father's body was stretched out in the driver's seat with the door wide open. His body was riddled with bullets, and blood dripped out. One of his legs was hanging out as his gun lay across his chest with his finger still on the trigger. His body poured over to the passenger side, and I didn't see my mother. Blood leaked from his mouth, but I couldn't focus on that. I needed to see my mother. My heart stopped. My father was the first dead body that I had seen, I was numb, but I needed to see my mother. I tried to climb over my father's bloody body, but they pulled me back so the people could lift him from the car.

"DOA," I heard one of the officers say.

It broke my heart to witness them pull my father's bloody body out of the car. My father wasn't a big nigga, but he was tall. They laid his body on the pavement to inspect it. As they handled him, my eyes shot back to the car. My mother was in the passenger seat with her AK on the side of her. I watched her stomach rise and then fall. She jumped up, grabbing her rifle.

"Where the fuck is my kids?" She had a faraway look on her face that I would never forget. She wasn't herself. She was in shock. Her pupils were dilated. I climbed into the car to rub her arm and get her to focus her eyes on me.

"Momma, I'm right here. Put that away." Her eyes met mine, and just like that, she was back in mommy mode.

She didn't put her gun down, but she spoke. "Get ya, brother, and let's get back to the house," she said, getting out of the car.

I went to Jahari, grabbed his hand, and went back to her. She grabbed my hand and picked Jahari up, putting him on her back as we walked away from the scene like nothing happened, and we hadn't discussed what happened since.

CHAPTER ONE
CURRENTLY

My ears started to ring. I couldn't hear shit. I didn't blink. I had to be tripping. Everything was good before we left. I had to be fucking dreaming. My eyes couldn't focus on anything but my fucking wife. I could believe the words that came out of my fucking mouth. The fucking phone call. This shit wasn't supposed to be happening. We were on the other side of the fucking world, and my son was fucking dying. I couldn't even fucking protect him.

"Look at me, Mahsyn." I blinked rapidly as I saw her face and remembered what the fuck was going on. This nigga Khap was tripping if he thought I was leaving my fucking wife in his care.

"Go ahead and handle yo business. I'll send her home when I think she ready."

Who the fuck this nigga thought he was talking to? My neck cracked as I turned it from left to right, never taking my eyes off her.

"Nigga," I got out before I upped my gun and started walking. No sooner than I did that, I heard guns clacking and bullets in the chamber.

"You take another fawking step, and you die, my brudda," Khap told me, and I knew shit wouldn't be easy.

Every nigga and bitch that I saw in passing was standing behind me with their guns drawn, ready to blow my shit to shreds. I wasn't pussy by a long shot, so Nobby had to know I would go out, guns blazing, behind her. I noticed Khap's hand sliding up Nobby's thigh. I knew she had a gun there. I wanted to fuck this nigga up, but we were outnumbered. We wouldn't make out this bitch alive if the wrong move was made. I watched as he pulled the gun from between her legs and lifted it in the air.

His wife turned to me. "We won't hurt her." She gave me a smirk, nodding her head toward the money. "Go help yo' son and take your money back. We got what we want, and your guns are being shipped as we speak. If not, this will end badly for you." She ran her hand down the front of my wife's dress, and I wanted to air this bitch out.

My mind went to a faraway fucking Candyland, and I didn't give fuck if we had to go out like Romeo and Juliet minus the drugs.

"Mahsyn, what the fuck happened to our son?" Zenobia jarred my thoughts. She was talking like these niggas didn't have guns pointed at us from every direction.

"Eyes on me. Fuck these foreign niggas. Now, tell me what the fuck is happening at home." She didn't flinch when she said it. Her poker face was on, and her only concern was MJ.

"No heartbeat," I told her, and I watched my wife deflate before my eyes.

It was killing me that I could get to her. There were two niggas guarding her. I was fucked up. I didn't know how the fuck we would get out of this shit, but she refused to fucking fold, and I wouldn't either. We had weathered many storms together, and this was just something we would look back on for years to come and laugh about with our grandkids. I didn't see the shit, but I had to hype myself up.

"Hold the fuck up. Y'all having a gun party and forgot to invite us. The fuck going on here?" I turned around, and this nigga Khaza was coming through the door with a gun bigger than his fucking body. Endymion, Bear, and a few of my niggas from the A walked in with him.

"Who the fuck are they?" Khap nodded.

Everyone was silent. I was shocked as fuck that they followed but thankful. Khaza shot the first nigga.

Blaow blaow.

Then, he turned to the other niggas and shot them down. Bear stepped over the dead bodies and started shooting shit up with Endymion.

"What the fuck? I thought this shit was just a gun exchange. And what the fuck this rasta-looking nigga doing close to yo' wife like that?" Khaza asked, and I didn't have an answer for him.

"Don't ask no questions. Khap, you have shooters, and so do I. We doing body for body now?" I asked him, and he grinned a little too hard for me.

"The only body I want is the one that you can't get to." He grabbed the back of Nobby's neck and licked the side of her face. I knew she wanted to vomit, but she remained trained on me.

"Fuck you, nigga!" I belted.

"Nah, but Imma fuck yo' wife," he said, and that was all I could take.

I put my gun down and walked over to him. Just as I was about to choke the fuck outta him, my wife stopped me.

"Magnolia, stop." I paused as if in a fucking trance.

"Go check on our son. I'm good. You gotta trust me."

I looked at her like she was fucking stupid. If she thought I was about to leave her with this crazy ass Haitian nigga, she was fucking crazy. She cocked her head to the side like she knew some shit that I didn't.

"Go and take them with you."

I wanted to protest, but what could I do except listen? My heart was breaking in two different pieces, and I didn't know which way to choose.

"Man, come on. They ain't gon' hurt her. Haitian or not, they ain't that fucking stupid. Let's go check on your son. Nobby straight."

Khaza grabbed my shoulder, but my feet wouldn't move. I didn't like this shit at all, but what other choice did I have but to beat my fucking feet? I sure hoped that Zenobia had a fucking plan because, for once, I didn't have a plan B.

She nodded for me to leave, but I refused to turn my back on her. She smiled wickedly as she watched me backpedal out of the room. The door closed once we were all out, and I turned to them.

"Where the fuck did y'all come from?" I asked them as we walked out.

"Nigga, when they made yo' private jet, they didn't stop making them. I knew some shit was off and acted on it, and I'm glad I did."

We walked out the back door with all eyes on us.

Once we were out, we separated and agreed to meet up once I got everything situated at home. As I got on the jet, I said a quick prayer for God to spare my son and Kadafi's life because if this nigga set me up, I was about to send him and his entire fucking family to hell.

I knew Zenobia felt hopeless because she couldn't leave

with me, but she remained focused. My mind went all over the place at the fucking thought of what Khap would do to my fucking wife. I would rather die than have this nigga put his hands on her. I pulled out my blunt from earlier and faced the entire thing. This flight would be long, and I needed to get my mind right in order to handle what the fuck was to come because this nigga had just started a fucking war that I hadn't prepared for.

Shit just wasn't adding up. I went over everything in my head, and I knew Kadafi wouldn't play on my top like that. It wasn't how he moved. I had been dealing with this nigga for years, and he never crossed me on shit. I needed all my shit together before I went in for the kill. I couldn't erase the look on Nobby's face when I repeated the message Lexington had told me. She was a mother first, and I knew her mind was noodles because of MJ. Her face spoke volumes that only I could hear.

Nobby would do anything to ensure the protection of our kids, and that was one of the many reasons I loved her. I knew she didn't want me to leave without her, but what other choice did I have? I needed to get this shit handled, but I had to see what the fuck was up with my son first. I dozed off from the blunt, thinking about how my life had spiraled out of control in just a few weeks, and I didn't think I could do this shit without my wife. God had to be trying to teach me how something I cherished the most could be swiped from under me so easily, and I was starting to feel just what he was trying to show me.

After what felt like forever, the plane finally landed, and I was relieved but almost fucking sad because I didn't know what I was about to walk into. I had broken my phone, so I had no communication after that one phone call, and honestly, I didn't want to know. The blunt had worn off, and I needed something stronger than weed to get me through this shit. I wanted to go straight to Kadafi, but I had to make sure my son was straight. There was a black Tahoe waiting for me as I walked down the strip. I hopped in with a heavy heart and a fucked up mind.

It took us twenty minutes to make it to the house. The entire house was solemn. I stood at the foot of the steps on the outside, and my heart dropped. For the first time in my fucking life, I was scared of what was on the other side of the fucking door. My head fell. Heart throbbed. I could feel that shit thumping outside my chest. My wife was out of the fucking country being held hostage and couldn't be by my side when all this shit was happening. I knew I was about to crash the fuck out, and no one would catch me. I couldn't cry because I had no more tears left. All I had was anger.

"Nigga, we wouldn't let you do this shit alone. We got you. We here for a reason," I heard.

When I turned around, Endymion, Bear, and Khaza were behind me, but Endymion was talking.

"We gotta handle that shit with Kadafi, but this is more pressing. I could have gone to that nigga's crib and blew that shit off the planet, but I didn't want to cause a fucking war, not that I give a fuck." That was Khaza's wild ass.

I shook my head because, for once, he used his head and didn't pop off.

"Thanks for that, but we will see that nigga very soon," I said just above a whisper.

I had to collect my thoughts for what the fuck I was about to walk in on.

I made my way up the stairs with my niggas behind me. When I tugged at the doorknob, the door opened. The women were in a line with their heads down, but I didn't see Lexington. They said nothing. All their heads rose when they heard me walk in. Khency, Janiya, and Yhental were the first to see me. Then, the nurses were standing there with defeated looks on their faces. It was true. My fucking son was gone. They didn't have to say it because it was written on their faces. Sorrow, gloom, sadness, and sympathy described what I felt inside.

"Where's Nobby?" Khency asked Endymion as he made his way to her.

I couldn't answer her. I felt helpless, defeated even. I had always saved Zenobia from shit, but this time, I couldn't. I knew she could handle herself, but I didn't know how those niggas got down in Haiti. The nigga didn't look like he would hurt her, but at that point, I didn't know who I could trust. I couldn't bring myself to say anything, and I knew Endymion wasn't about to open his mouth. I ran my hands over my head because I couldn't bring my mouth to say shit.

"Where is my son?"

I looked around at them, but the only eyes that met mine were Janiya's. Bear hadn't made it to her yet. Tears ran down her cheeks as she looked at me, shaking her head from side to side.

This shit couldn't be happening. My fucking son couldn't be dead. This was not how this shit was supposed to go.

"Where the fuck is my son?"

I felt my anxiety getting the best of me. They were being too fucking quiet. I walked through them because I needed answers, and they weren't going to provide them. I took the steps two at a time until I got to the suite where my son was. I paused before I went in to mentally prepare myself for the unexpected.

I pushed the door open and walked in. Lexington was standing over MJ's body. The machines were still hooked to MJ as Lexington stood over him, looking confused. I walked and stood next to him as he looked down at my son. MJ looked lifeless. I rubbed his arm, and it was cold and hard. I wasn't the smartest nigga in the world, but I knew he must have been dead. The machines were literally keeping him breathing.

"I asked you to guard my fucking son with your life. To choose staff who could care for him and keep an eye on him in my fucking absence. I haven't been gone a full two days, and this shit happened!" My hands went around his fucking neck. I watched his light skin turn beet red as I choked the life out of him.

"What the fuck happened to my son? I left him with you because I fucking trusted you, and you failed me." I gripped his neck harder.

He tried to speak, but nothing came out because he was gasping for air. I didn't give a fuck. My son's life was just about gone, and I didn't have the answers I needed. I was slinging his body all around the room because I had no more fucks to give. I was running out of options. My life was falling apart, and I couldn't control it.

"Nigga, if you let him go, maybe he could tell you what the fuck happened. He can't talk if you are holding his windpipe hostage," I heard Endymion from behind me.

I had checked out. When I looked into Lexington's eyes, I saw that he was clinging to life by a thread. I turned around, and Endymion and Bear stood in the door, pleading with me with their eyes to let the man go. I turned his ass loose, and he fell to the floor with a thud.

"Man, stand the fuck up and tell me what the fuck happened to my son. Give it to me straight, no fucking chaser."

I didn't give a fuck that he couldn't breathe. If he didn't give me honesty, breathing was the last thing he would have to worry about. I watched as he tried to catch his breath and stand to his feet like a man. He stumbled back a little so he could explain.

"I don't know what happened. Everybody was on their respective shifts. Everything was moving fine. He even started to breathe without the machines, but then last night, the alarm went off, and I rushed in here where the nurse was performing CPR. He was still on the nasal cannula, so I didn't understand how his heart just stopped."

I replayed everything that he had told me in my mind. I didn't want to think the worst, but the worst had already happened. What they didn't know was that I had cameras all over this motherfucker and would find out if he was telling the truth or not.

"Where were you when all this shit was taking place?" I asked him.

He looked into my eyes. "I couldn't get too much sleep, so I had been in here even when the nurses were in here, making sure everything was okay. He started to stir like he was in pain, and then he started to pull at the tubes. I knew he was coming out of the coma, and I wanted you to know. I stepped out of the room, but before I could get to my phone, the alarm was going off with a code blue. I knew how I left him, so there was no way he could have stopped breathing in seconds. His eyes were open. He was looking for you," he told me, but something still wasn't adding up. He was alert but then stopped breathing all in the same minute.

"What fucking nurse was in there before you left my son's room?" I asked.

He stood silent like he wasn't a snitch. He didn't know who he was fucking with, but I was about to show him.

"Endymion, take Khency, Yhental, and Janiya to the other side of the house. I don't need them to know what the fuck we about to do," I told them without turning around.

"Oouuuueee, we about to have some fucking fun," Khaza's trigger-happy ass shouted.

Endymion did as I said, and Khaza stayed in the room with us. I walked over to my son's bed and looked down at him.

"I know you still in there somewhere and can hear my voice. You will come back from this shit one way or the other." I kissed his forehead and looked at the doctor.

"You better fucking fix it, or you gon' get what the fuck I'm about to do to your nurses who decided to mistreat my fucking son." I walked away from him, and my niggas followed me out the door.

I then walked back down the stairs where the nurses still stood. They didn't have the fear of God in them, but they would need it for what the fuck was about to happen if they didn't speak up.

Zenobia didn't know this, but I had bought a building in the middle of the grimiest part of Buckhead. I always knew one day that space would be beneficial, and the time had come. It looked like an abandoned building, but it was really my own personal mortuary. Everything was brand new, down to the floor.

I didn't think I would have to use it because I had left that life alone, but as usual, the time had come for me to put my skills to work. I looked around at the nurses, reading each of their faces. Nothing stood out. Their faces didn't hold any lies, but I knew someone was responsible.

"Nigga, you taking too fucking long. Staring at these bitches like my nephew ain't laid up in the fucking bed. Which one of you nurse bitches wasn't paying attention to my fucking nephew?" Khaza came from behind me with his gun in his hand. He aimed it at each of their faces.

"We can do this the easy way, and someone speaks up, or

we could play innie minnie minnney mo. I don't give a fuck. All y'all bitches can die," he said, walking around them.

They still didn't say shit. Khaza only put fear in them but really didn't want to say anything because he talked with his guns, and now wasn't the time for that. I looked at them as Khaza pointed his gun in their faces with Bear not too far behind. Then, I noticed it. The one who didn't show any remorse for what happened to my fucking son. She stood, not moving, ready to meet her fucking fate, but I had other shit in mind for her.

My brain went into overtime as to why she did the shit and how the fuck she knew me. I wouldn't point her out because then her cover would be blown. The more I looked at her, the more the pieces in my head started to come together. Her features were of a Haitian woman, but why target us? Was this shit pre-planned, or was I really slipping? All the questions swarmed through my brain like a hive of honeybees. I didn't want to crash out and fuck up more than I could handle without my wife, but I needed answers.

I slowly walked over and stood in front of the Haitian bitch. I folded my arms across my chest to try and threaten her, but she didn't flinch. This bitch was willing to die for her fucking family before she told me what the fuck was going on. Since she wanted to play the fucking mind games, every nurse was about to suffer for her silence.

"Man, fuck all this dumb shit. Endymion, go get the fucking covers. Khaza, keep an eye on them, and Bear, you roll with me. We about to take them to my mortuary and see if they gon' talk when we get there," I told them, and the niggas looked at me like I was crazy.

I had to keep a special eye on Khaza because that nigga was a younger version of me, and I knew he would blow their heads back if I turned my head.

"Y'all gon' see when we get there," I answered before they could ask what the fuck it was.

It was really self-explanatory, but they were about to see why niggas in New Orleans called me the Grim Reaper.

When Endymion came back with the bags, we put them over their heads, tied their wrists together behind them, and walked them to the waiting black Sprinter that I had parked in the back of the house. I knew my fucking son wasn't dead, and foul play was involved, but I needed answers, and one of those nurses knew what the fuck was going on. We had to drag them because they refused to walk, which was fine with me. We jumped in the Sprinter and headed to our next destination.

After driving for about forty-five minutes, I turned the lights on in the Sprinter and pulled up behind the building. From the outside, it looked like a haunted house, some shit you saw in a scary movie, but the inside was immaculate. All my tables and equipment, such as machetes, steel tables, and the morgue, were brand new. I had everything looking good for times like this. The slabs were in a row for decapitation and cutting of the body parts, and the furnace to turn them to ashes wasn't too far away.

It was soundproof, so any screaming wouldn't be heard. It wouldn't be anyway because the hood was loud as fuck. A gunshot was like a ringing fucking doorbell where I had this house. On the second floor was where I tortured motherfuckers if they got out of line. I had chains hanging from the ceiling with a tarp on the floor because I hated my floors to get dirty.

"Nigga, what the fuck is this?" Khaza asked. "This nigga on some Halloween H20 shit, and I'm fucking with it, but what we gon' tell our wives when we get back?" he asked.

I chuckled because Yhental had his ass scared. With the

shit I knew about him and what he did, this nigga should not be scared of a woman.

"Nigga, I know Yhental lil' ass ain't got you geeking. Nigga, you did shit that I wouldn't even think of doing, but I get it. This shit gon' be quick and easy because I think I know who the nurse is, but I'm trying to figure out the fucking why. Why would she target my family?" I told them, and they all looked confused. I would have to explain that part to them later, but right now, I wanted action.

"Look, they know what the fuck we do and how we do it unless y'all niggas keep secrets, but I don't keep shit from my wife, so let's go," I said and hopped out of the Sprinter with them following close.

I lifted the trunk of the Sprinter, and we all grabbed the women. We dragged them, kicking and screaming, to the back door. I unlocked the bolts, and we dragged them to the second floor. My adrenaline was high because I hadn't had to get my hands dirty in a long time. We stood them in a line, and Khaza went behind them, yanking the bags off their heads one by one. That nigga got a thrill from it because he was trying to take their heads off with each one.

I looked over at my table. A rifle, machete, a few bricks, scalpels, and rope. My shit was prepped for surgery. I made sure all my men had their overalls, surgical masks, and boots ready to put on over their clothes. We didn't need blood splatter on our clothes. I was already stressed the fuck out, and these bitches weren't making it any better. They stood off to the side as I made my way to the table to grab my machete. I knew this bitch was on to something, but I needed to know what before I tortured her. I usually didn't kill women or kids, but this bitch was being too quiet, and for that, her coworkers would suffer right along with her. The only difference was they valued their lives, but she didn't. That shit didn't surprise me at all because bitches like her were willing to die for the code of silence.

I pulled the string to turn on my machete and noticed Khaza smiling. This nigga lived for shit like this, but it was my turn. I walked back and forth in front of them, smelling their fear.

“Which one of you bitches was on shift when my son coded? And please don’t fucking lie.” I looked into each of their eyes. They should have known by then that they weren’t making it out of there alive. They didn’t say shit.

“Khaza, grab the fucking chains since they don’t wanna talk.” I watched Khaza move. “Maybe being hung from the fucking ceiling will help their fucking mouths move.”

I nodded to Endymion, and he assisted Khaza. I knew a little about Bear, so he got the chance to sit back and watch the fucking show. Even with the shit in Vegas, I paid attention to him and knew he wasn’t a hothead but a silent killer. I admired that about him. Khaza and Endymion lifted the ladies and hooked them to the chains with their feet dangling over the floor. All the women were in fear except that one, and I was about to find out why.

I stood before them as they hung from the ceiling with tears rolling down their cheeks. I could have stripped them naked, but I didn’t want to humiliate them. It was enough that I had to kill them and go against my rules.

“Which one of you motherfuckers were on fucking shift when my son coded?” I asked again, and no one said anything. I locked eyes with the bitch who didn't show any fear and walked toward her.

“It’s you, right?” I looked at her name tag. Tawanda. A unique name for a fucked-up woman. “What the fuck you did to my son, bitch?” I was trying to be nice to the bitch, but she wasn’t making it easy at all. Instead of answering me, she spit in my fucking face. Khaza sprinted past me with his gun in hand, ready for action.

Blaow, bloaw

was all I heard as he knocked them bitches' socks off. When I got to the one next to Tawanda, I told him to stop.

"Nah, they look alike. They gotta know each other, so they gon' get tortured together," I told him, and he paused.

Bear was being quiet as fuck, and that was to be expected.

"Bear, let them dead bitches fall to the floor, and clean this shit up. Fuck the clean-up crew."

He got right on it like I knew he would. The nigga was quiet but deadly.

Endymion, you see that radio over there? Turn that bitch on. I got surround sound in this bitch, and I need to concentrate," I told him, and he cocked his head to the side at me.

"The fuck you need music for, nigga?" He laughed as I chopped ole girl's foot off and watched it roll to the floor.

I couldn't tell him the music made me feel closer to my wife. Like she was standing next to me. She was screaming and snotting all over the fucking floor. Feces and piss reeked in the room. Thank God we had our Pooh Shiesty masks on.

"Nigga, just hit the play button," I told him and waited for the music to croon through the speakers.

There's no reason why we should be apart
Mmmm, Oh baby
Cause searching for something out there
Will lead two lonely hearts, two lonely hearts
(Baby, don't you know)
We come too far to let it all end
I've told you over and over again
How I feel inside but if you go
Oh baby, there's something you should know

Something you should know.
There's something in my heart my mind boof
(Something in my heart, something in my heart)
Ooh, has got me hooked on you

Zenobia loved that song, and I needed it now more than ever because she wasn't with me. I was trying my best not to let that demon of those pills take over, but I needed them. I needed to get in touch with my nigga and have him drop me a few to take the edge off. I knew I shouldn't have, but I needed it.

"Now she fucking scared. She can't even hold her fucking bowel movement. That shit hurt, huh?" I asked her, and she still didn't say shit. The bitch on the side of her was begging her to tell the fucking truth.

"Just tell him what the fuck going on, Tawanda!" she screamed, but I didn't give a fuck because they were gonna die anyway. She didn't have on a nametag, but I knew she had to know something.

"How about you fucking tell me since you seem to know? And where the fuck is my music?" I yelled, but the bitch didn't say anything. That further pissed me off.

"Khaza, shoot this no-name hoe." I nodded toward her, and he blew her head off her body.

"And then there was one. You better get to talking because if you don't, your body parts will be floating in the river, and yo' family will never find you. I gave yo' ugly, duck-looking ass a pass for spitting on me because you a female. I kill niggas for less than that on a good day, so be careful with what comes out yo' fucking mouth." I stood in front of her with my machete in my hand.

I was over the talking back and forth; I needed answers. Her screaming was starting to irritate me. I walked as close to her bloody body as I could without getting any on me. I walked around her body, taunting her. This was the shit I missed.

"Bitch, you either gon' tell me what the fuck you know and why the fuck my son was in your care and damn near died, or I'll cut your tongue out, and I'll make sure you feel every part of it." I chuckled as her body shook.

I knew I didn't have much time because I hit a main artery in her foot, so it was only a matter of time before she bled out. I didn't want that. I wanted to further torture her until she begged for her life, and I got my answers. She hawked a mouth full of blood at me, and I jumped back just in time. She smiled, and her teeth were bloody.

"Your son is already fucking dead, motherfucker," she spat at me.

I wanted to blow her shit back, but I had to think smart. I didn't believe a fucking thing she said. My son wasn't fucking dead.

"You think so, but I know the difference, bitch. Now tell me what you fucking know."

Before I could get my last word out, Khaza came from behind me with his gun in his hand and put it to her neck.

"Bitch, tell my brother what the fuck he needs to know, or Imma blow yo' fucking thoughts to the wall. Fuck all this talking shit." His hostile ass didn't have patience. I didn't either, but I needed her to give me something.

"If you kill me, you really won't get the answers you need." She laughed, and I laughed with her.

I grabbed Khaza's shoulder, pulling him back. I knew he was ready to kill her, but I needed to know some shit before he fucked it up. A dead body couldn't speak.

"Chill, nigga, I got this. Get the cleanup crew to clean this shit to help Bear with the rest of these bitches. I got her," I told him.

He rolled his eyes and walked away. I brought my attention back to her, and she was still smiling. Her face made my ass itch, and my hands itch even more because the bitch thought it was funny. I raised the machete to her neck and asked her one final time.

"What fucking part did you have in playing with my son's life?" I stated as calmly as I could because I was losing it. I revved my machete up, ready to chop her ass into pieces.

"Ask yo' brother," she said faintly before I let my hands do the talking and split her body in half.

I didn't give a fuck that her blood was all over me. The words that came out of her fucking mouth fucked my head up. What the fuck did Jahari have to do with my wife being in Haiti and my son being fucked up?

I walked away from everybody and out of the warehouse with them silently behind me. Bear already knew to call the cleanup crew to take care of shit. I walked to the truck and hopped in on the passenger side because I was too stuck to drive. They got the hint because Bear hopped in the driver's seat, and the rest got in the back. The entire ride was silent, everyone in their own thoughts. I didn't know if those niggas heard what the fuck I heard, but the state was about to bleed once I got to the bottom of why people chose to fuck with my family. I was trying to do shit the right way, but that wasn't working, so it was time for me to put in work.

Once we pulled back up to the house, I jumped out before he could put the truck into park. I walked into the house and told my guard to bring me every piece of camera footage from every angle since I left. Then, I walked up the stairs, bypassing my son, and went straight to the suite that I shared with my wife. When I walked into the room, everything was still how I left it. I could still smell her natural scent of vanilla and coconut in the room. I wanted to fuck shit up, but I knew I had to be strong for her because she would do the same for me.

I pulled my clothes off as I walked into the shower. I looked at the mirror and pictured her standing there, trying to see how she looked in a tight-ass dress. I shook my head. I needed her back already. If that nigga knew what was best for him, not a fucking loc on her head would be out of place. I hated that I had to kill a woman because that's not how we moved, but it had to be done.

The words of that lady still lingered in my mind as I took out the clothes that I was wearing for the day and stepped into the shower. As the hot water ran down my body, I placed my hands against the wall. My mind was in shambles because I didn't know what the fuck to do without my wife. We were both the brains behind everything, and half my heart was halfway across the earth.

I closed my eyes and let the water run down my body as I planned my next move. I needed to get this nigga Trahan and see why the fuck he wanted my son dead so bad. My mind went to Daisy and what the fuck she was doing fucking with my son. I had her hiding in the shed behind the house, but I had two guards watching her, making sure she was straight. It was something about her that made me feel like she was genuine, but her connection to Trahan and Lotus still had me looking at her sideways. That, and his family trying to take over the United States, but Daisy was different because I didn't know her motive.

I needed my wife for all this shit because I couldn't do it alone. I felt the water getting cold, so I turned it off and got out. Grabbing a towel from my warmer, I wrapped it around my waist and walked into our bedroom to get dressed. I pulled my Polo boxers and wife beater on and opted to wear a pair of Balmain jeans and a shirt with a pair of matching Jordans. I didn't know what the day would bring, but I was ready for it. I grabbed my .45 off the dresser, tucked it away, and went downstairs to meet my brothers.

I knew in my heart that my son wasn't dead, and I bypassed the middle floor so I wouldn't have to visit that part of my heart. I made my way downstairs and was greeted by Bear, Endymion, and Khaza. They, too, had changed into their street clothes and looked like they were ready for whatever.

"What the fuck that bitch told you? Because you ain't said shit since we left," Endymion asked me as I walked with them, following me to my bar in the living room. I needed a few shots because the shit she said didn't make sense. I threw back two shots of Don Julio before giving them the answer they had been waiting for.

"The bitch told me to ask my brother," I told them, and they looked just as confused as I felt.

"The fuck she meant by that? Jahari didn't have anything to do with MJ or Zenobia," Bear asked.

"Zenobia because she was fucking Haitian," I told them and slammed my fucking shot glass on the table.

I needed to call Jahari and tell that nigga to make his way back to fucking Georgia because I needed answers from him, and I wanted it face to face. Too much shit was going on, and my life felt like it was crumbling, but I wouldn't let it. Endymion stopped me by grabbing my shoulder.

"What we gon' do about MJ? You need your mother now more than anything, nigga. It's time to face facts," he told me, but I didn't want to hear that shit.

I couldn't accept what the fuck was going on, but I knew I would have to.

"He good for right now, nigga. I needed to find out what the fuck was going on with my brother," I told him and got up to use the phone in another room. I dialed his number, and he answered on the second ring.

"What's good, nigga?" he asked.

On any other day, I would laugh because he was so corny, but today, this wasn't that.

"Stop whatever the fuck you doing and hop on the jet and get here. No excuses. We got shit to discuss." I disconnected the call and waited for him to come because I knew he would be here by tomorrow.

I needed to know what the fuck was going on.

CHAPTER TWO
KADAFI

"Fuck, Makeda, do that shit just like that. Be a good girl to Daddy," I whispered, pulling my wife's hair back to watch her give a nigga some of that million-dollar mouth.

"You sure you can handle it, Daddy?" She moaned against my shit, making it jump.

I hadn't heard from Magnolia since I hooked up the deal with him and that nigga Khap, so I assumed everything went smoothly. No news was good news. I had to call him, though, because he wasn't a quiet nigga, and he was being too quiet. Khap hadn't reached out to me yet either, and that nigga was worse than Magnolia, so something had to be wrong. I would wait for one of them to reach out because I didn't want to get in the middle of what they had going on. All I did was make the introduction and went over the exchange. That was it.

I didn't find it strange that Khap wanted Magnolia to come all the fucking way to Haiti to give the payment, but Magnolia didn't say shit, so I didn't either. We were all grown men who moved differently. I just hoped everything turned out okay because they were both hotheads.

I had taken Makeda out for the day, and we ended up at Spades strip club. That's what I loved about my wife. When I first met her, she was on her shy shit, but she slowly blossomed into my little freak. She didn't give a fuck where we were; if she wanted to get sucked and fucked, then we were doing it wherever we were.

We had gotten dressed and went to the steak house for dinner and drinks. I had to handle some business, so I dropped her off at the house while I went to handle shit. I didn't want to hear her mouth about me always leaving the house, so I made sure that I wasn't gone too long. Apparently, I was gone long enough because when I walked into the house, it was dark.

Candles illuminated the entire walkway. Rose petals made a trail to our living room. I followed the trail, and it led me to the dining area. There was a big oak table with six chairs surrounding it. Music was faint in the background, but I heard the words loud and clear. I looked up to where the roses were, and there Makeda's thick ass was. She was sitting at the head of the table with a pair of ten-inch red bottoms on. Her legs were wide open with each foot on the table. She had my favorite Gucci bomber jacket on.

She stood to her feet, and my mouth watered. Makeda had shaken the thickness off her waist, even though I loved that shit. She worked out three times a week and ate all the right foods. I was proud of my baby, but I vowed to fatten her ass right back up. Her thick, hourglass figure, along with her bow legs, walked over to me as the music faded in the background. She got close to me. With her heels being high, she was almost to my nose. She grabbed the back of my head, pulling me down to kiss her lips.

I sucked her shit like my life depended on it. I was obsessed with my fucking wife, and she knew it. My hand palmed her ass cheeks and lifted her in the air. I walked us back to the chair, and I sat down. My dick poked her middle. I looked down at what she had on, and my dick grew bigger. She had on skintight boy shorts and a black lace bra that was covered by my jacket. It turned me on seeing her in my shit. She was on demon time because my wife was usually very reserved, but I liked this freaky shit.

"What you doing, mama?" I asked, gripping her hips.

"I'm about to show you how I ride, but first," she said, hopping off me. I slid the chair back. "I wanna taste you."

I didn't know what the fuck came over her, but she was feeling herself, or maybe it was the fucking drinks. She squatted between my legs and used her mouth to pull my zipper down. She winked her left eye at me and pulled my dick out. Nah, that wasn't gon' work. I needed to be butt-ass naked for this shit here. I pushed back, stood up, and took all my clothes off in one swift motion. I then sat back in the chair, and she grabbed my dick, gobbling me down. I bit into my bottom lip because her jaws were suctioning my shit.

"Fuck..." I felt the frown on my face as I watched her give me sloppy. I taught her everything she knew, but this shit was something new.

"The fuck, Mak?" I called her by her nickname.

I was about to nut, and I didn't want to. When the tip of my dick hit her tonsils, I knew I was gon' nut before I got in the guts, and I wanted to taste her. I grabbed her hair and pulled her to me, giving her a sloppy kiss.

"Good girl, but it's my turn," I told her and lifted her onto the table.

I pulled the jacket and bra off, and her breasts sprang from her bra.

"Lift up," I demanded, and she lifted her ass from the table.

I pulled her shorts off, and her legs gapped open. Her hairless pussy stared at me. I could see her juices glistening all around her southern lips and slit. My mouth watered and got dry at the same fucking time. My eyes traveled up her body, and I didn't know where I wanted to suck and kiss first. Her body was perfection at its best. She licked the tip of her finger, hypnotizing me.

"It's your world, Daddy. You know I just live in it." She made me feel like the fucking king I was. I was just missing my crown. I sat down in the chair, spreading her lips to my liking.

"Look me in my eyes while I devour you," I told her and sucked her clit.

She hissed like a snake. My tongue moved like a snake as I put my entire face in her pussy. She was losing control, and that's how I wanted her. She could never handle my mouth.

"Daaamnnnnn," she moaned but kept her eyes on me. One hand was on my head, and the other pinching her breasts.

"Nah, I got that," I hummed.

My hands slid up her body and grabbed both her breasts. I wanted to cater to her body until she couldn't take it anymore. Her clit swelled, but I didn't want her to bust on my face. I stood and rubbed my dick on her slippery opening. I used the back of my hand to wipe my mouth because she had soaked a nigga.

I slid in inch by inch until I filled her up. Her back arched off the table as I stroked her slowly. I wasn't in a rush. I wanted to hit every corner. I pulled out and licked her pussy again. She moaned loudly and tried to push me away.

"Move yo' fucking hands, Makeda," I told her, and her eyes sprang to mine.

She knew when I was in my zone, I didn't like to stop. She slid her hands up to my chest and held on for the ride. In and out, her pussy sucked me in deeper and deeper. My head fell back.

"Eyes," she told me, and I yanked my head forward.

I looked down at our connection and knew I was about to nut deep inside her. I picked her up from the table with my head in the crook of her neck, kissing and sucking, leaving marks along the way. I turned her around on all fours atop the table and smacked her ass.

"Arch your back," I told her, and her shit was the perfect shape of a U.

I bent down and bit into her ass cheeks, one then the other, before I stood and slid back in. I didn't know what music was playing, but the sound of it made me slow and then quicken my pace.

Step 1 bite this
Don't make a sound until I let ya
Step 2 I'll lick that
Tie you up so you can't run
Step 3 on my knees
Turn my face into a seat
Step 4 let it go
Let it drip down on my tongue
It's time to make a movie
Have some fun go get your toys
Got some pop rocks and the cough drops
You know exactly what for
Better answer when I call you
Yea you're daddy's nasty
With every stroke, I hear you ask me
Why you doing me like this
I know you like it Nasty (I know you like it Nasty)

The nigga who was singing that made me wanna do all the shit he was talking about to my wife. I stroked her until she was begging me to stop, but that still didn't stop me.

"I'm about to bust. This shit so warm. I could live in it forever. You the shit, girl."

I had to give praise where it was due because my wife had the best pussy in the world, and I couldn't deny that. I wasn't a fucking saint, but if I could do shit all over again, I would have skipped all the hoes I had and met her first. Makeda was my everything, and I would shake the world for her.

"Do that lil thing you do." I smacked her ass, and she looked back at me.

She licked her top row of teeth and blew a kiss at me. She was throwing her ass back in slow motion while making her cheeks jump one at a time, driving me crazy. My knees buckled as I stood there and let her do her thing. This was our favorite position because we both fought to control the other. She tightened her muscles while throwing it back, making the tip of my dick extra sensitive. She knew just what Daddy liked. My nuts tightened as her walls sucked my dick. Just as I was about to let loose inside her, my phone rang.

"No, keep going, baby. I'm almost there. Please."

She knew I was going to stop because my motion stopped. Fuck, I was about to nut too, but I needed to take that phone call. It was my street burner ringing, so I knew it was important. She continued to throw her ass back at me, but I gripped her hips to stop her.

Without pulling out of her, I reached over for my pants and pulled my phone out. It was Magnolia calling. Yeah, I had to take this. I answered the phone as I still made love to my wife.

"What's up, nigga?" I said, trying not to sound like I was fucking.

"Nigga, climb out the pussy and meet me at my house, cuz

we got some shit to discuss." With that, he disconnected the call.

I didn't like his fucking tone and the way he dismissed me like I was a young nigga who he was grooming.

"Who the fuck was that?" Makeda asked.

I tried to keep her away from my street shit because I didn't want her tainted, but she wasn't blind to it. I was still stroking her, and we both nutted. Finally, I picked her up from the table with her legs around my waist and carried her to the bathroom.

"That nigga Magnolia got some shit going on with him, and he wants me to meet him at his house," I told her. I was glad we lived in the same state because I wasn't getting on a fucking plane.

"Am I going with you this time or sitting this one out?"

Makeda was so fucking pretty when she really wanted something. She batted her eyelashes as she stared at me. She was so fucking submissive, and that shit was a turn-on from the beginning.

"Nah, you rolling with me because I need to see what this nigga talking about." I left her with that because my mind started to wonder what the fuck was going on.

CHAPTER THREE
JAHARI

"What's going on, bae?"

Amerika was in my ear, but I didn't feel like hearing her fucking voice. This shit was her fault, but I couldn't place all the blame on her. This shit was all on me. I couldn't even be mad because I brought all this shit on myself. Had I listened to my first fucking thought, I wouldn't be about to be at odds with my fucking brother.

Growing up, I knew that this wasn't the life for me. That's why I always took the high road and let Magnolia handle everything. But, this time, it was on me. Magnolia had always come in and saved the day, and I had to save his when I touched down. I knew that phone call was coming, and I also knew what this conversation was going to be about when I landed in Georgia.

"We gotta back up and head to Georgia to talk with Magnolia," I told her in haste because I knew she was about to be on some bullshit.

"We just fucking left there. What the fuck he gotta say face to face that he couldn't tell you over the phone? I'm tired of the fucking back and forth. I know he got shit going on with MJ, but we got a life, too," she said.

I turned to her, grabbing her neck. She knew I didn't play when it came to my fucking family. I squeezed the front of her throat.

"I don't give a fuck how you feel at this point. You can stay the fuck here. I didn't ask yo' ass to come," I told her, and she sank her teeth into her bottom lip.

I was being serious, and she was thinking about fucking. That was her, though. She liked when a nigga got rough with her. It made her think about the times when she used to be in the club and I slutted her ass out. The shit was comical.

"You know I'm rolling with you, but first, I need to roll on this dick." I hated when she got like that because everything else clouded her judgment.

"Stop playing, Amerika, and pack yo' shit to meet with the fam," I told her, and she chuckled, rubbing my chest.

We'd just hopped out of the shower and were about to get dressed to go see about our dispensaries in Los Angeles. It was time to pick up money, and I had planned to take her out on an early dinner date before coming back home. That was until Magnolia called me with his bullshit. I knew what it was about, but I wouldn't tell Amerika. We were just getting back to a good place, and I wasn't trying to fuck it up.

She slid the towel from around my waist. Her small hands wrapped around my girth, and I sucked in air. She knew just what to do to make me forget about what the fuck was going on. I threw in my gangsta card the minute I started fucking her in my strip club.

"Fuck, man, you not playing fair." She started stroking my shit, and my head fell back. Her tongue licked the base of my neck, and I knew it was over.

"All is fair in love and war." She sucked where her tongue was, and it was over.

I swiftly picked her up, with her hair falling all over my face. My dick was brick, and I needed to feel her. Fuck the foreplay and shit; I wanted to fuck, and she did too. Her eyes told it all. Slanted, low, and hypnotizing. I held her in my arms, and we never broke eye contact. I gripped her thighs, sitting her on my dick, inch by inch. We had been married for years, and she still had to adjust to my girth. Her arms wrapped around my neck as her lips connected with mine. One hand controlling my head and the other around my neck, her tongue filled my mouth. I sucked on her lips as she began to roll her hips on her own. Her shit was so warm and tight that I almost burst prematurely. She slow winded on me, and my knees buckled.

"Can't take this pussy, huh? Still folding after all these years of getting it." She was talking her shit, and I can't lie, she was telling the truth. Her pussy had me under a spell that I couldn't shake if I wanted to. I felt my knees buckling. "Sit down," she told me, but I wouldn't fold.

I had to take control of the shit so we could go. She was trying to make love, but we both knew we wanted to fuck. Her whispering those words in my ear gave me all the ammunition I needed to bounce her ass up and down on my dick. I tightened my arms around her body and started bouncing her. I wouldn't tap out because I knew that was what she wanted.

"Umm, fuck..." escaped her lips as her head fell back.

My lips went to her neck and sucked while I fucked her into an orgasm. My nuts got tight, and I knew my dick was about to spit gold.

"Nah, talk yo' shit. You had so much to say when you had control. Now, you squirming. Take this dick," I growled in her ear, and her body shuddered.

Sweat coated her back as I dug deeper inside her. She

moaned everything I wanted and needed to hear in my ear. Her hands met each side of my face as she kissed me long and hard. My duck jumped, and I started moving her up and down at a fast pace until my nut shot inside her. I stood still until I was empty, with her clinging to my body for dear life. Both our bodies were soaked with sweat as her hair stuck to my shoulders. After a few minutes, I let her feet down to the floor, and she stood on wobbly legs. She looked up at me, smiling, and I couldn't help but smile back because she had that effect on me. Amerika was the most beautiful woman in the world to me, and it would kill me if she ever left.

We took another shower, and she dropped to her knees, blessing the mic, of course, before we got out and took care of our hygiene. While we were getting dressed, I looked at her through the mirror. I knew she wanted to ask me something, but her mind was holding her back. It was strange, though, because my wife didn't hold shit back when it came to me. I knew I'd fucked up and was making up for it, but she was holding onto something, and I wanted to know what it was. The worry lines on her face confirmed that she was walking around with a heavy heart, and I couldn't have that. I didn't know what the fuck I was walking into fucking with Magnolia, but I needed her on her A-game when we touched down. We hadn't been home a full week, and this nigga was summoning me back to Georgia like it was a short drive.

"What's up, Amerika? Talk to me. You know we never had a problem communicating, so don't start that shit now," I told her as I pulled my wife beater over my head. I was dressed comfortably because I didn't know what the fuck was going on.

"I haven't talked to Zenobia since we left, and my heart is telling me that some shit ain't sitting right, but why is Magnolia calling you to come all the way back to Georgia? We just left there, and everything was good. Is everything okay? What did he say on the phone?" She was shooting off questions, but I could only answer one at a time.

"I have no idea why he wants to talk to me. Knowing him, it's probably something that could be discussed on the phone, but you know how this nigga is. He hates discussing business over the phone. As far as Zenobia, have you tried calling her? She is dealing with a lot," I said, and her head sprang up. I knew she was about to start talking crazy.

"Don't you think I have been calling her? Her phone keeps going straight to voicemail. Shit don't feel right. I know she be pulling a lot of hours at the hospital, but after the shit that happened on New Year's Eve, I don't think it's work that's keeping her from answering the phone," she told me, moving her head around with an attitude.

I hated to ask her about anything concerning her friend because she held her on a high ass pedestal. I threw on my Gucci tracksuit with my matching tennis shoes. Then, I sat on our bed and watched her get dressed. Even in the most comfortable clothes, my wife was fine as fuck. She sat at her vanity, using some type of blowing machine to dry her hair. She was dressed in a pink Gucci maxi dress that hugged her every curve. On her wrist, she had on her Cartier watch with her clover bracelets to match her dress.

I loved her hair in the straight state. It made her look like a sexy vixen. Once she finished with that, she slid her perfect pedicured feet into her Gucci slides and got up to walk over to me. She stood between my legs, grabbing my face for me to look at her. My hands ran down the side of her body, trying to deter my mind from flying across the country. She grabbed my chin, and I looked up at her.

"Don't do that," she told me, playing in my beard.

"Do what?" I asked.

“Don’t shut down on me. Just like you pay attention to me, I do to you because you are my soulmate, so tell me what the fuck is going on, Jahari. Whatever it is has you bothered, and I need to know because you know how my mouth can get behind you. I would go to war with the fucking wolves behind you, but don’t let me go in blind, baby.” Her voice was soft, but I couldn’t tell her something that I didn’t know my fucking self.

“I really don’t know why this nigga wants me to come, but I have to. I don’t wanna call my mother because she probably doesn’t even know what the fuck is going on. I didn’t wanna seem like a fucking momma’s boy because I call her for everything, so I’ll see what’s up when I get there. I really don’t know what’s up, baby. You know if I knew, I would tell you. I’m walking into this shit blind, just like you,” I told her, standing to my feet and pushing her back a little.

“Are we packing anything?” she asked as she grabbed her purse and iPad. I knew she would get some reading done while we were on the plane.

“Nah, anything we need, we’ll get out there. It might be an overnight trip, so let’s just head out so we can come back.” I grabbed her hand and led her out the door. I had my car service take us to the strip, so we could get this shit over with.

As we sat in the back seat, my mind wondered what the fuck was so urgent that he needed my presence instead of a phone call. This nigga must’ve thought I lived up the street. Granted, we had a private jet, but I was trying to get our lives back in order. All our businesses were legit, so I was confused about what the fuck he wanted. I couldn’t refuse to go because then he would come to California, and it wouldn’t be a friendly visit because of the shit he had going on. He would’ve fucked me up for sure. I needed him to be focused on his son, but he always had some shit going on.

Growing up, Magnolia was always my protector. I didn't have to worry about anything happening to me, and I knew it was a big job for him as a kid. I didn't ask for protection, but after our father was killed, Mhyesha instilled in us to always protect the other, but more so, Magnolia protected me because I was a little soft.

I wasn't soft; I just didn't like drama. Magnolia didn't either, but he was a different type of man. He'd been that way since Mason was killed. I believe it was then that his mind went to another fucking dimension, and he didn't give a fuck anymore. He killed without a conscience and would fuck bitches to calm his adrenaline. My mother tried everything when we were coming up. Doctors, meds, even some type of psychotherapy, but that shit only made it worse. Mhyesha just let him be him because she couldn't control him. I loved my brother no matter what and would stand with him in whatever he did.

"Stop at Starbucks before we get on this plane because I'm hungry." Amerika snapped me from my thoughts and returned them to her.

I leaned forward, tapped my guy's shoulder, and told him to stop at the nearest Starbucks by the airport. I was starting to get anxious over what the fuck was about to happen. I had a feeling it wouldn't be good. My driver stopped at the Starbucks, and I hopped out of the truck to go around and open the door for Amerika. If I hadn't, she would've never gotten out. I opened the door, and she stepped out and kissed my lips, winking her eye at me. She knew I wasn't coming in with her, so she walked away, and I watched her ass bounce up and down. She turned to me, and my eyes met hers.

"Whatever you think it is, it's not, so stop internally stressing about shit you can't control and let shit be. Whatever it is, we will handle it together. Do you want your regular?" she asked me with a smile. My wife knew me better than I knew myself sometimes. She knew when I was stressed or worried about something. I nodded my head up and down. "Nah, you can finish watching my ass as I walk away," she told me.

We both chuckled as she disappeared inside the store. I took that time to think about everything that had transpired over the years. I was thankful for everything I had and will get in the future.

"Stop staring into space and open the door." Amerika walked up to me with everything in her hand.

I had zoned out, but I quickly recovered and opened the door for her. She got in, and I went to the other side to hop in. She handed me my iced mocha latte and my buttered croissant. The smell made my stomach growl. I hadn't realized how hungry I was. I looked over at her and realized she had some type of frozen coffee shit with whipped cream spilling over the top, a croissant, brownie, and some other type of pastry. I just watched as she set all the shit on the seat and started sipping her drink. Her eyes met mine.

"The fuck you looking like that for?" She sipped her drink, picked up her brownie, and devoured half of it.

"You had to get all that shit? You act a nigga starving you or some shit."

She said nothing but kept eating. I shook my head.

"I'm hungry, Jahari. You just knocked the Mario coins out of my pussy, and I'm hungry." She chuckled with food in her mouth.

I just sat and observed her. When I was in the pussy, it was extra warm and tight as fuck. I knew she wasn't cheating or no shit like that, but she was warm as fuck. I licked my lips, thinking about the shit. Her ass might have been pregnant, but I would keep that part to myself until we got back home.

We made it to the private airway, and I got out to open the

door for her. She grabbed all her shit and hopped out of the truck. I wrapped my arm around her thick hips as we walked toward the plane. My mind was heavy, but my heart was even heavier because I knew it would be some shit when we touched down. I felt that shit in my soul, but I was ready for it.

After what felt like hours, the plane was finally about to land, and Amerika had fallen asleep. I nudged her, and her eyes opened. She looked at me as crumbs fell from her lips.

"We here already?" she asked, looking around.

I nodded my head up and down. We waited for the plane to become steady before we took our seatbelts off and got off the plane. I looked out the window and realized there was a black Tahoe with limo-tinted windows waiting for us. I couldn't see if someone was in it or not. There was a guard standing on the back side of the truck, waiting for us to get off. It seemed odd, but I didn't say anything.

We stepped off with Amerika in front of me. When I reached the bottom step, the back door of the truck opened and out stepped Magnolia. He was dressed in a trench coat with dark-colored shades hiding his eyes. Something was off about him, but I couldn't read him. My brother always exuded power and never displayed weakness, but it was written all over him. He was battling internal shit, and I knew it would be hard for him to tell me. It was always like that growing up.

Magnolia always took the brunt of everything because he was a protector. The one time I needed to be there for him, I couldn't be because he wouldn't let me inside that part of his brain. I wondered if he had talked to Mhyesha, but the way he looked, I knew he hadn't because he usually only told her what was necessary. I walked over to him.

"What's up, bruh? Why the impromptu visit?" I asked as I held my hand out to dap him up.

He looked at my hand like it was shit, but I didn't trip. I

didn't know what the fuck was going on, but I was eager to find out because he was acting salty as fuck.

"Damn, Magnolia, was all that necessary? Where is my friend? Why is she not with you? I have been calling her phone, and the shit is going straight to voicemail." Amerika stepped in front of me.

I knew she would speak because his attitude was off. She was the Bonnie to my Clyde. Magnolia pulled his glasses off, and his eyes were bloodshot red. I knew he was fucked up from the faraway look in his eyes. He wasn't stable, and something had happened.

"Let's talk about this shit at the house." He walked away from us and went to hop back in the truck.

The ride back to the house was quiet. Every now and then, Amerika would cut her eyes at Magnolia. She was clearly itching to say something but kept her mouth closed for the sake of peace. I grabbed her hand, giving it a little squeeze because I knew she was ready to shake shit up. Magnolia hadn't answered any of her questions, and we all knew how she felt about Zenobia. Shit was fucking with her. I silently thought about Zenobia, too, and where the fuck she was. Magnolia didn't move without her at his side. Some shit had to have happened, and it had to be serious for him not to be able to speak about it until we got to the house. I knew the beef with those Chinese motherfuckers was taking a toll on him because of MJ, but that was lil shit to a giant. Magnolia would pack up the fucking military and blow China to shreds behind that shit with his son.

Once we got to the house and inside, we went straight to the bar area. There was a couch and a TV. The setup was like something in a movie. Amerika and I sat on the couch together as Magnolia walked over to the bar and poured him a shot. Yeah, this nigga was about to flip the world upside down. This nigga had potato sacks under his eyes, so he wasn't getting any sleep. His beard was wild, making him look like a psych patient. He had mentally checked out.

"Nigga, what's up with you? You ain't said shit since the airport. You look rugged as fuck, and I have yet to see MJ or my sis in law, so what the fuck is really going on? Is there something I need to fucking know?" I was irritated because the tension in the room was so fucking thick that a knife wouldn't cut through it. I didn't know if I was the reason for the fucking problem, but his silence was killing me bad as fuck.

"Calm yo' fucking tone with me, nigga. You don't know the shit a nigga been through because you ain't never had to do the shit I had to do, so wait until the fuck I answer you. This past couple of fucking days have been rough on me, so excuse my fucking attitude. But don't come in my fucking house, thinking you gon' talk to me any type of way because it's nothing for me to fucking kill you, brother or not, so slow the fuck down," he barked at me.

I knew this nigga was bugging. He had never talked to me like that. I could have kept the shit up, but clearly, this shit was bigger than me, so I didn't say shit.

"Magnolia, just tell me what the fuck is going on. Why you make me fly from Cali to Georgia to have a conversation that could have been over the phone. What's up, nigga? This me you talking to," I told him in a calmer tone.

He looked at me with tight eyes. "You sho this a conversation you want to have in front of your wife?" he asked, throwing back another shot.

Now, I was really invested. I never kept secrets from my fucking wife, and she was rolling her eyes at me. She let go of my hand and moved further away from me on the couch.

"I ain't going no fucking where, so you might as well get to fucking talking." America rolled her eyes at me as she stood up.

She walked over to the bar where Magnolia stood and grabbed a shot glass. She poured her own poison and took it to the head. "Because I feel like this shit got something to do with my friend, and I need to know what the fuck is going on. Magnolia, I feel like you beating around the fucking bush with information, and you know how I feel about Nobby. I didn't miss the puffy fucking red eyes, and your entire demeanor is different, so I can answer for my fucking self. I ain't leaving this fucking room until I know what the fuck is going on," Amerika told him and poured another shot.

I guess the shot glass wasn't big enough because she jumped over the counter, got a glass, and put ice in it. She then poured more of the Julio into her glass, filling it halfway. I didn't want her drinking so much because she got crazy when she drank brown, but it was too late. She was already fucking the drink up.

I got up from my seat because I knew if she was staying for this conversation, I was gonna need plenty of shots.

"We got one more guest before I even talk about this shit because it's all twisted, and I ain't trying to fuck up by killing my brother or the nigga I'm trying to do business with," he said. I remained quiet because I knew he wasn't gonna kill me. It didn't matter how mad he was; he was just talking shit. "I ain't trying to turn the entire country into a fucking blood bath."

Now, that, I could believe because when that nigga's superpower was turnt, he was a fucking force, and Nobby not being here would make the shit worse. My brother had officially lost his fucking mind. It was gone. I didn't miss the wild look in his eyes that he tried to cover up. I would bet my last dollar that he was taking them fucking pills again because he wasn't himself.

Something happened when I left, and I didn't know what the fuck it was. I knew the kids were with Mhyesha, so my mind ran rampant on what the fuck was really going on. I knew MJ was upstairs, probably healing, but where the fuck was Zenobia? And what was this nigga not saying? Before I could open my mouth to say something else, the door chimed.

Magnolia pulled his phone from his pocket to look at the cameras. He chuckled before walking toward the door, leaving us to drink. After a few minutes, he walked back toward us, and I had to blink twice. I hadn't laid eyes on this nigga in years, and I didn't know my brother was doing business with him. I knew he was looking into gun selling, but I didn't think he would fuck with him. This nigga matched my brother's crazy, so them two together were a dangerous pair.

"Kadafi, what the fuck you got to do with this shit?" I asked him.

Magnolia looked at me, shaking his head from left to right as if to keep quiet.

"Nigga, mind yo' business," was all he said.

"Nigga, don't answer no questions because one of you niggas is the reason my fucking wife is being held against her fucking will in a third world fucking country, so let's play a fucking game of we listen and don't judge. What the fuck happened?" Magnolia pulled his rifle out and put it on the fucking counter. I didn't even know where that bitch came from. I knew sugar was about to go to shit because he meant business.

"Somebody is fucking lying, and I need some answers," he said.

I closed my eyes and prepared for what the fuck he was about to say.

CHAPTER FOUR
ZYRESE

I didn't know what the fuck was going on. I don't do much noise, but I knew MJ was home and we were no longer going on vacation. I always listened before I spoke some shit. It fucked me up that Trahan was the cause of my family being torn apart and MJ being in a hospital bed at home, fighting for his fucking life. That's not how this shit was supposed to go. I didn't even know where my sister put Daisy, but I knew she was probably mentally fucked up because if nobody knew my sister, I did, and when she got mad, she opened hell's gates.

I was ready to go back to school because staying in that fucking room all day and only coming out to eat wasn't it. The one time that I snuck into MJ's room, I couldn't handle seeing him hooked up to all those machines, so I didn't go back. That fucked with my heart because I loved him like a brother.

My mind drifted to Nobby. I hadn't heard her voice around the house, and I knew she was on vacation from work. She and Magnolia had business to handle, but that nigga came back without my sister and didn't tell me shit. That was a problem for me because although I knew he loved me like a son, he wasn't my sister. If something happened to her, I didn't know what I would do. She was my person and would forever be that. I had autism, but I wasn't stupid. I was smart as fuck and knew when shit wasn't right, but I didn't speak on it.

I grabbed my iPad and began to finish the picture I had started of the girl at school who I had become obsessed with, and she didn't even know it. She was beautiful. She had long, silky hair that she kept in a ponytail. Her eyes were slanted but big, covered by the longest lashes I'd ever seen, and they were natural. Her button nose matched a set of juicy lips, and the color of sun-kissed caramel skin made me feel things that I'd never felt.

We had a couple of classes together, but she never noticed me because I always sat at the back of the class and was the last to leave. Her smile was contagious. She had to be raised wealthy because she kept all the latest shit on. Gucci, Fendi, Yves St Laurent. She even had a fucking G-wagon that she drove around in. I watched her every day as she got in her jeep with her friends and left campus to go wherever. She lived on campus—that much I knew because I would stay outside until she returned. I even started to follow her to make sure she got inside safely. I wasn't stalking her; it was more about valuing her safety. I missed doing that shit, and it was driving me insane that I couldn't be at school.

I wasn't scared of Trahan. He knew exactly who the fuck I was, but what he didn't know was what the fuck I was capable of doing. Magnolia keeping me locked in this room like I was fragile was crazy work. He trained me on how to defend myself with or without a gun. I knew he was keeping some shit from me, or there was more to the story, but he knew what would trigger me. I couldn't control my shit. That's why I never carried a gun. I wasn't afraid of them; I just didn't like the sound they made. This is the reason I have a black belt in karate and know how to defend myself without a weapon. My hands were lethal but gentle.

I continued to draw my dream girl with my AirPods in my ear, listening to Kendrick Lamar's latest album. I was trying my best not to let my thoughts get the best of me, so I remained quiet. I reached over to grab my phone and pressed Nobby's name to call her, and it went straight to voicemail. I had called her over a hundred times since she left with Magnolia. I didn't want to ask too many questions because of the shit that was happening with MJ.

In their absence, I heard the machines blaring one night but didn't think too much of the shit because it didn't last long. If Magnolia had motherfuckers in his house and around us, then that meant he trusted them with our lives.

I couldn't focus on that shit too much because I had other shit on my mind. I knew that whatever was going on with my sister, she could handle it because Zenobia was strong. Nothing could shake her, not even Magnolia, so I knew in my heart that she was good. I was focused on MJ getting better and getting back to school to my dream girl. I may have become obsessed with her and didn't know her name. All I knew was that her hazel-colored eyes had hypnotized me into delirium, and I had to check on her to make sure she was okay.

We had been in this house for almost a week, and I felt like she needed me in some sort of deranged way. I removed my headphones because I thought I heard voices. I thought everybody went their separate ways after the whole ordeal because Magnolia had officially lost his fucking mind. There was additional security around the house, but I didn't feel like the nigga was coming back. He had done enough damage to last us a lifetime. I got up from my bed and went to my door to get a better listen.

"What the fuck happened?"

I didn't recognize the voice, but I knew it wasn't Magnolia's.

I used that as my opportunity to grab my duffle bag and leave the house. I knew Magnolia would be distracted by the talk that was happening, and my personal guard was cool as fuck. He told me if I wanted to leave the house, he would take me where I had to go, so I was good. I was ready to get the fuck out of this house and go where I was comfortable—my room at school.

Grabbing my duffle bag and my iPad, I left the room. I bypassed MJ's room, but I had his car keys in my pocket because I was gonna duck security too. I had changed my mind, and I didn't want him to take me. I knew how to drive myself back to school, and I would handle the other shit once I got there. My only problem was getting past Magnolia's gigantic ass unseen.

Once I got to the bottom step, I knew they were in the living room, and I had to pass it to get to the front door. I thought about going out the back door, but the guards would alert him, and I wasn't about to fight through those big niggas. I kept my head down as I walked through them, but all the talking ceased when they saw me.

"Nigga, where you going? I told you it ain't safe for you to be leaving the house with all this shit going on," he said as I looked around at everybody in the room.

I recognized everybody except one couple, but it wasn't my business to ask who they were.

"You know I can handle myself," I told him with my whole chest out.

He looked at me sideways.

"I want to go back to school. Classes already started, and

I'm trying to graduate on time." I was giving any excuse to get the fuck out of there.

"You got yo' gun on you?" he asked.

I didn't, but I couldn't bring the shit to my room.

"I do, but I don't need the shit because my hands are lethal, and you know this." I put my hands up like I was about to fight. "I have MJ's keys, so I'll just take his car." I reached into my pocket and pulled the keys out to show him the key fob.

"I have eyes everywhere, but let me holla at you for a minute." He grabbed my arm, ushering me away from everybody else. We walked into another area, and I stood in front of him. Something about him was different, but I wouldn't bring it up.

"How close are you with that nigga Trahan?" he asked me.

I thought about lying, but that nigga would know.

"I just know he came after MJ because of Daisy, but he ain't never saw me and MJ on campus. He likes the way I draw, so we started talking through that. You know how I am with certain people," I told him because I was non-verbal to strangers, but Trahan was cool.

He stepped closer to me. "You can go back to school but act normal. The nigga knows you related to me and probably thinks MJ is dead because shit is quiet, but this shit is bigger than a bitch," he told me, and I didn't want to know the rest.

I wanted to ask him about Zenobia, but I knew he would tell me if it was something bad.

"Just be you. Don't let shit change. See what's up with that nigga but don't volunteer any info, just listen. If the nigga moves different, then you know what to do. Get to know that nigga and his family but don't be pushy. Do what I taught you, and at the right time, bring that nigga and his father to me, so I can show him what hurt feels like. You have every number that you need in your cellphone. If you need anything, don't be afraid to use it." He dapped me up and walked away.

Magnolia didn't know I had my own shit up my sleeve for that nigga. If that nigga breathed the wrong way, Magnolia ain't have it worry about me bringing him. I would kill them niggas myself. I knew what I could and couldn't handle with autism, but what I didn't do was give two fucks about ending a nigga's life.

We walked back into the area where everybody was, and I noticed my iPad on the sofa face up with my dream girl on the screen. Before I could pick it up, Magnolia grabbed it and inspected the picture.

He looked at me. "Who the fuck is this? Do you fucking know her? Have you seen her before? Because you know how the fuck your mind works."

The way he said it had me wishing I had kept my shit in my hand. I grabbed it from his hand and looked at him. His eyes were slanted, and I knew he was about to say some slick shit.

"She goes to my school. No, I don't know her. I barely know her name. I just see her around campus and follow her sometimes," I told him and laughed.

"Oh, so you a stalker now? You like her or some shit?" he asked, and I felt my cheeks get hot.

I didn't want to tell him because of the face he made when he picked my shit up.

"Nah, it ain't like that. I just think she's pretty. That's it," I half lied because I wanted her to be my wife.

He smirked at me. "Get to know her. See what her name is and let me know how it works out. That needs to be done because she looks familiar as fuck," he said and walked away from me.

I let out the breath I was holding because I thought he was about to tear into my ass. He always treated me like I was handicapped, but I wasn't. A nigga just liked to draw. I waved bye, went to the car, and left the house without looking back.

It took me forty-five minutes to get back to school, and I was excited because it was my norm. It was where I felt most comfortable. I pulled up and noticed everybody walking in their own zone, minding their business. I got out of the car with my stuff and went to my room. Because I was autistic, my shit was private, and I could do what I wanted in that bitch as long as I went to school every day.

The apartment was still on campus, but it was separate from the other dormitory. Magnolia had shit set up that way because I loved to draw with loud music late at night. Sometimes I would stay up until it was time for me to go to glass, drawing shit on my canvas or on the walls. It just depended on my mood. It was cool with me because of the privacy. I hit the locks and started my walk to my apartment when I noticed her. I felt saliva form in my mouth, and all the blood rushed to my dick as she walked casually with her friends, talking.

I was stuck. I wanted to go over to her and say something, but I didn't know what to say. I stood there, watching her smile and laugh at something that one of her friends whispered in her ear. The world stood still. My eyes didn't blink. I looked down at my watch and wondered what class she was going to. I needed to schedule my shit, so it was a chill day for me. I had my Black card in my wallet to order some food for my room, so I was good.

"Nigga, where you been? Oh, that's right. You were with yo' family." I felt a strong arm over my shoulder, but I knew who it was.

"Trahan, don't fucking scare me like that, nigga," I told him. I didn't give a fuck if he was Chinese.

"You looking hard as fuck at her. Why don't you go talk to her?" he said.

I turned for a second to give him a look.

"Nigga, you don't know who the fuck I'm looking at." I shrugged him off me because he was being too fucking nosy. "And what the fuck were you doing at my house for New Year's?" I asked him, and his entire facial expression changed. His smile was more like a scowl, but he tried to hide it. I caught that shit but didn't say anything.

"I was just in the neighborhood and saw all the fireworks." Now I knew the nigga was lying because we didn't do all that shit, but I would let him have that for now.

"Anyway, when did you get back to school?" he asked, and I dangled my keys.

"I just pulled up, nigga. Why?" For some reason, I was on the defense with this nigga since Magnolia told me to befriend him.

"Calm down, bro. It was just a question," he said, and I nodded. "Nah, seriously, you should go talk to her," he said, still talking about my dream girl, and I didn't like that shit. No one knew how I felt about her, and he didn't need to either.

"Well, there is a party tonight at the frat house, so come through. I know for sure she gon' be in the building because she is an AKA," he said, and I noted that in my brain because I just might slide through.

"Bet. What you about to get into?" I changed the subject because I wanted to know where this nigga's mind was.

"Nothing. About to head back to my room and get some sleep for tonight. Rese, you better come through," he said.

"I just might," I told him before rubbing my beard and heading to my room.

I had my head down, ordering food for my room because I knew my shit was empty. Just in case I didn't go to the fucking party, I would have some food and turn on Netflix and paint.

Ahhhhh.

That was all I heard before a crashing sound and books hitting the fucking floor. I didn't move. I looked up from my phone to see a girl on the floor with her head down. Hair covered her face as she tried to gather her books and the sack that had spilled all over the ground. She ran into me, and I didn't even feel her. Where the fuck did she come from? I thought I was walking alone. Not too many people resided where I did, so I was a bit confused. Maybe she was lost.

"Keep your head out your phone and pay attention. You don't own the sidewalk." She had an attitude, but the shit was sexy.

I looked closer at her and noticed it was my dream girl, but I didn't understand. She was just walking with her friends in the building, and now she was in front of me by herself. She raised her eyes to meet mine, and her hazel orbs hypnotized me. This girl didn't know the effect she had on me, and I didn't even know her name. My mouth wouldn't move. I wasn't in control of my body to even help her pick up her shit from the ground.

"Helloooo, are you even going to help me pick my stuff up from the ground?" Her soft, sultry voice snapped me out of my realm.

I quickly put my phone in my pocket and proceeded to help her. I reached for her hand, and when our hands connected, electricity shot through my body. It made me feel alive. I looked at her, and she must have felt it, too, because she smiled, and her teeth were perfect. Her smile was perfect. Everything about her was perfect.

I reached around her waist with my other hand and scooped her up to her feet. Once she was steady, I bent to pick up everything that had dropped with one hand while she held her bookbag. She held it open while I put everything back inside, but I noticed that her zipper was broken. It was some type of designer tote, so it surprised me that it was broken.

I took a minute to take her in up close. She was so fucking pretty. She smiled while swiping her hair behind her ear and stood there silently, probably thinking of her next words. I didn't want to say shit because I knew I would stutter, and the shit was embarrassing. I wasn't sure if I wanted to say anything at all. My lips were glued shut.

"Why do you live all the way over here? Are you disabled or something? You don't look like it," she asked.

I stared at her lips because I couldn't say shit. She stood there, waiting for an answer, but nothing would come out. I was pissed at myself because I had so many thoughts going through my mind that wouldn't reach my lips.

"You must be autistic and non-verbal, but it's okay. Thanks for helping me." She began to walk away, and I got nervous.

This was my only chance to talk to her, and I was fucking it up. She probably wouldn't fuck with me anyway because I was autistic, and she pointed it out without me telling her. I took a chance and grabbed her arm before she could fully walk away. She looked down at the arm I held and then at my face.

"You are either going to talk to me or let me go." She didn't say it in a defensive way but in a cute, girly way with a smile.

I blushed but didn't say anything. She threw her tote over her shoulders and came into my personal space. She grabbed one of my dreads and twisted it.

"It's okay. I'm studying psychology, and right now, I'm taking a class that deals with issues such as yours. So, when you are ready to talk, we can." She tried to walk away again, but I stopped her.

"Tell me what you're thinking. What's your name?" she asked, and I put my head down.

My dreads fell over my face because I couldn't answer her.

Her hand went to my chin and lifted my face to meet hers. She smiled, and I crumbled on the inside. Her eyes stayed on mine, encouraging me to speak.

"I stttuutteerrr when I tttaallkk to a sssttrraannggers," I barely got out in a low tone.

"I know that, but you will get to know me and feel comfortable." Her soft voice was like music to my ears.

"Zyrese," I told her, but I didn't stutter.

"Jadior," she said with a smile.

I didn't want her to leave just yet, but I didn't want her to see my apartment with the shit I had all over it. I knew I could get rid of the shit I had painted on the walls, but my easel and shit were still dirty, and I had tarp on the floor.

"Let me gggett you another bbbbagggg," I stuttered, and she smiled.

"Your stuttering is actually cute, but you don't have to get me another bag. That's what I get for being nosey, anyway. Do I look like I need you to buy me another bag, Zyrese? I could buy another one myself." I gave her a confused look. She noticed it and went on to explain. "When I was with my girls earlier, I saw you before you saw me. You pulled up fast in that Camaro, and I wanted to see who would get out of it. I love fast cars." She blushed. It was the cutest shit ever. Her cheeks turned beet red, along with her smile.

"We slowed our pace, and when you got out of the car, my friend whispered in my ear that you were my type, and I laughed."

I thought back to when I saw her laughing. Good to know they were talking about me.

"I didn't know that you were autistic," she said, and I got offended. "But that's okay because you are my type, and I am not judgmental because we all are flawed." I noticed the sad look on her face, and I suddenly wanted to fix it, but I didn't know the story behind it.

"Where is your phone?" she asked, and I pulled it out of my pocket.

I wanted to say more, but I wasn't a pushy ass nigga. I wasn't used to interacting with people outside of my family, especially women. I reached into my pocket and gave her my phone. I didn't have a lock code on it, so it opened right up.

"You were ordering groceries, I see. I want something." She smiled, and I shrugged.

"Order what you want, but it's gon' come to my room," I told her.

"Or how about we just go to Walmart? It's right up the street, and I am finished with classes for the day."

I didn't know how to answer that because she was stranger danger. Something about her told me that she was genuine, and I knew if need be, I could snap her neck with my hands, leave her ass on the road, and call Magnolia, so she was better safe without me, but she insisted.

"Come on. I want to take a ride in your fast car."

Before I could answer, she grabbed my hand and dragged me back to the parking lot and to the car. I hit the locks and opened the passenger side door for her because I was a gentleman. She slid in with ease, and I closed the door, went to the driver's side, and hopped in. I revved the engine and pulled out of the parking lot. I looked to my left and noticed that nigga Trahan smiling wide as fuck, giving me the thumbs up. I was glad she didn't see that shit, but I would ask her if she fucking knew him, and if she did, it would break my heart because that nigga was a snake.

For the first few minutes, the ride was quiet, so I decided to ask a question because the silence was killing me.

"How am I your type?" I knew it was random, but that was the first thing I remembered her telling me.

She looked at me, and I glanced at her, then back at the road. She was fiddling with her fingers and her head down.

"Don't shy away from it. It's just you and me in the car. No one else will know what we talk about," I assured her, and she gave me a half smile.

"Well..." She reached over and grabbed two of my locs. "Looks can be deceiving because, my first look at you, I thought you were a bad boy because of the jeans, chains, and your demeanor. That's my type, but when I ran into you on purpose, I knew you were different," she said and laughed.

I knew already that she was affectionate because she couldn't take her hands off my hair.

"That's the image I give? That's not what I am, though," I told her.

"I see that now," she said.

"So, does that change your attraction to me?" I wanted to know.

"Not at all. It makes me want to know more about you, Zyrese, because I know that mentality lives in you. You just haven't tapped into it yet. I know you're related to MJ, right?" she asked me, and I was surprised because we barely hung around each other because he was usually with Daisy, and I didn't want to be the third wheel.

"Something about you is different, and I want to explore that."

I didn't like the fact that she knew so much about me that I hadn't even mentioned. I didn't even know her.

"How do you know so much about me?" I asked her as I pulled into the parking space at Walmart. It wasn't too far from campus.

"Just like I know you been watching me for some time now,

I have been watching you. Now, let's go make the groceries because I already know what I want," she said as I put the car in park and went to the other side to open her door.

We walked around the store, and I was surprised when she grabbed my hand and put her head on my arm as we walked through the store. She picked up a few things that she wanted, and I grabbed the things I needed, and we made our way to the checkout line. I didn't get much because I didn't eat pork, and I survived off noodles, Powerade, and cookies, but I also got my mac and cheese and other things I needed outside of food. Everything came up to over $500, and I was cool with that. I pulled out my Gucci wallet and gave the cashier my card. She was looking at me like she knew me, but I knew she didn't.

"Why you looking at him like that?" Jadior said to the cashier, rolling her eyes.

I wanted to laugh, but I kept my cool.

"He for you or something? Because he fine as hell," the cashier said, still looking at me.

I heard Jadior smack her lips. I guess she was waiting for me to answer, but I didn't because I didn't know her, so I wasn't saying shit. Jadior smiled because she knew why I wasn't answering her. She took the card from my hand to give to the cashier.

"Sweetie, he will not answer you because he is mute. Here's the card." She pushed the card to the cashier's hand, and she took it.

The cashier was still looking at me, and then she rolled her eyes at Jadior. I didn't say shit.

"Do you want to keep yo' fucking job, or do we need to go to another fucking line? I gave you the payment, but you ain't made a move yet." I couldn't believe she was talking like that, and the shit was awakening shit in me that I didn't know I could feel. The shit was turning me on real bad.

"I'm sorry. I didn't know," she said.

"Don't worry. I didn't know either, but I know now, and so do you, so can you check us the fuck out."

The girl hurried to tap the card and put our groceries in the basket.

As we walked out, I laughed my ass off because she was walking fast as fuck. I watched her bowlegs walk to the car and stand by the trunk to wait.

"Slow down, beautiful," I told her, and she looked at me. "You acting crazy to say you barely know me," I said as I popped the trunk and started to load the groceries in. She went to pick something up, but I stopped her.

"Nah, I'm a gentleman. I got this. You just stand there and look pretty," I told her, and she smiled.

"Where are you from with that accent? I didn't miss that and the fact that you're talking to me without stuttering. You must feel comfortable around me now, huh?" She came over and kissed my cheek.

I didn't know how to react, so I kept my cool.

"I'm from New Orleans, baby," I told her, and she giggled.

"I knew you were from the dirty south," she said, but I didn't respond.

After I put the groceries in the trunk, I went to open the door for her to get in. She turned around to face me and rubbed the side of my cheek.

"You gon' be my husband," she said and got in the car.

I couldn't help but blush as I walked over to my side of the car and got in. I didn't say much else during the ride back to campus because she had declared how she felt. What she didn't know was I was ready to propose and didn't know shit about her.

CHAPTER FIVE

JADIOR

I never thought the shit would be like this. I knew who Zyrese was the day I realized he was watching me. He had been watching me since he stepped foot on campus, but I never thought he was autistic. He really didn't know who I was, but I had him right where I wanted him. Everything I told him was true. I was studying psychology, and I knew autism when I saw it, but he was different. He looked different from the usual autistic people that I have come across. I also knew he was sheltered from a lot of the shit his sister and her husband did, and it showed.

I looked at him as he maneuvered through traffic like he owned the street. That shit was a turn-on, but I wouldn't let him know that. Zyrese was sexy as fuck, and I knew it wouldn't be hard for him to fall in love with me because he was already there. It was only a matter of time before we were together, but I would take my time and get to know him.

My parents told me all about Magnolia and Zenobia and how they believed that Zenobia killed my sister, Dior. They expected me to find out whatever information I could so I could prove that she killed my sister. I was against it at first, but my mother told me to go after the weakest link, and that was Zyrese. He wasn't the weakest link, but I knew I could get to him instead of Magnolia because he didn't let anyone near him but his wife, so I knew that was a no-go. Zyrese was someone I knew I could manipulate with the right strategy and have him eating from the palm of my hand.

I could almost bet that he was a virgin because I never saw him with any female on campus, so I knew it wouldn't be hard for me to get to him. Now that I had talked to him and knew the things I knew, I had a change of heart, and it hadn't even been twenty-four hours. I wanted to call my parents and tell them no, but I knew they would cut me off if I did.

I had a lot riding on finding out who killed my sister. I didn't give a fuck about who killed her. She always fucked her patients and bragged about it, thinking the shit was cute. My parents didn't know what she was doing, but I did. Dior used her prettiness and her sex appeal to break up happy homes. Sometimes, that shit worked, and the last time cost her life.

I wasn't into all that shit. I only went to school for psychology because I wanted to learn the mind. I didn't want to be a fucking therapist. If I did, I wouldn't be a marriage therapist. My parents thought I was the black sheep of the family because I lived by my own rules. As soon as I graduated high school, I didn't give them a chance to give me a party before I was gone. All I wanted to do was get as far away from them as I could.

They were obsessed with how Dior died, and I was over it. I don't know how they got the info on Magnolia and his wife, but they told me they wouldn't pay for my college education unless I got close to their family. They knew every fucking thing. I knew I couldn't talk to MJ because he had a girlfriend, so my next step was Zyrese. He was the easy target. I knew I couldn't hurt Zyrese because he was innocent, and he was sexy as fuck. I genuinely wanted to get to know him, and if it slipped out, then it did. But until then, I wanted to get to know him.

I looked at his side profile as we drove back to campus and parked. He was so handsome, and I wanted to see what his apartment looked like. I knew he had money because of how he carried himself and what he had on.

"We can bring your stuff to your room, then I got my shit from here," he told me, and I felt defeated. I wanted to see the inside of his apartment, but he wasn't having it.

"You must not want me to see your apartment, but I get it because you don't really know me anyway," I told him, and he just looked at me.

We were back to the silent treatment. I took that as a yes and got out of the car before he could come around to open the door.

"Pop the trunk," I told him when he met me by the back of the car.

He didn't say shit, and he didn't pop the trunk. I stood there looking at him with piercing eyes. He didn't budge. We were in a stare-off on how the groceries were going to get to the other place. He was funny, and I knew this would be fun.

"Just let me help you, Jadior," he said, sounding exhausted.

I gave in because I knew he really wanted to help me.

"Only if you let me help you," I challenged him, and he let out a sigh of frustration.

"Okay, bruh, you could help me, but let's bring your stuff first," he told me, and I smiled on the inside.

We took my stuff out of the trunk, and I led him to my

room. I lived on the third floor of the dormitory, so I was glad I didn't get a lot from the store. I really didn't need anything, but I wanted to get some time in with him. I didn't want him to come into my room because I had a roommate, and I knew she would fucking drool over him, but he was mine, whether he knew it or not.

When we got inside the room, my roommate was lying in her bed, half-naked, with the cover at her waist. Zyrese hurried to turn his head, but when she noticed I had a nigga with me, she got out the bed.

"Girl, put some fucking clothes on. I got company," I told her, and she smiled at Zyrese.

"Don't even think about it, bitch. I pissed on him. That's my territory, and he's a mute, so don't talk to him because he won't say shit back," I added.

Zyrese looked at me and laughed. He followed me to the kitchen and helped me put up my groceries, never taking his eyes off me. I didn't know how to feel about that. I didn't know if it was a look of admiration or dislike because his face was stoic. I would find out once we left there.

It took us a few minutes to put my stuff away, and I felt my phone vibrating in my pocket. I pulled it out and saw that it was my father. I wanted to ignore his call, but I knew he would keep calling back-to-back, so I answered.

"Yes, father?" I answered.

"Did you find out any information on Magnolia's family yet?" he asked.

I moved slightly away from him because I didn't want Zyrese to hear me.

"I'm working on it. You gotta give me a chance to see what's going on." I was trying to speak in code because Zyrese was watching me like a hawk.

"Well, if you don't get any information by summer, kiss tuition goodbye." With that, the phone call disconnected.

I wanted to throw my phone against the wall and crash it. I had to control my anger because I didn't want Zyrese to see that side of me. It was too early, and we didn't really know each other. He must have sensed my aggravation because he closed the refrigerator and pulled me to him. I was surprised because it was off guard. He wrapped his arms around me, pulling me in tight.

His head went to the crook of my neck, and he whispered, "Fuck whoever that was. I got you."

When he said that, he kissed the side of my neck, and my entire body tingled. He didn't know what the fuck he was doing to me, and I was bad for him. I was angry that I had to do this for my family, but I had to if I wanted to stay in school. I was too close to the end to fuck up now. I wrapped my arms around his neck and tried to keep my tears at bay because he didn't know the inner demons that I was fighting just to stay in school. I could have told him my motives, but the way he was caressing my back had me slowly melting like putty for him.

"Let's go," he whispered before letting me go.

We walked out of the room with me in front of him and his arms wrapped around my waist. I felt safe in his arms, but when he found out what the fuck I was doing, that safety net would turn into a raging inferno.

We took a quiet stroll back to the car to get his groceries. He had a little more than me, so I helped him carry his stuff, so it would be one trip. Once we got to his front door, he paused and turned to look at me.

"Don't judge me, okay?" he said, and I gave him the stink face.

"Trust me, I am the last one to judge anybody, but that's a story for another day," I said because I knew I would eventually pour my heart out to him. He turned and fumbled with the keys to open the door.

Zyrese walked in first, with me behind him. I was in awe. There was blue tarp covering the entire floor. He had four easels with paint and brushes everywhere. He had painted all over the walls, but they were beautiful pictures. Tribal prints, portraits of famous people like Beyonce, Ciara, Cicely Tyson, Malcom X, and even a female that I didn't recognize. We took everything to the kitchen and started to put the groceries away. He even painted on his countertops. This was his comfort zone, and he had let me into it.

"I know you probably think I'm crazy," he said as he put the food up.

I grabbed him and turned him to face me. "You can really paint, Zyrese. Why would I think you are crazy?" I asked.

"Some shit that I may tell you about me might make you wanna run for the hills," he said with a solemn look on his face. He had a story to tell, and in due time, I knew he would tell me because I wasn't going anywhere.

He had finished putting his things away, and we were now standing there, looking at each other.

"Well, that's it. You want me to walk you to the door?" he asked, and I acted appalled.

My hands went to my chest like I was out of breath.

"You putting me out already? What did I do?" I acted like I was hurt.

"Nah, I'm not putting you out, but I know you probably got other shit to do than to be here. All I'll do is paint until classes start," he told me.

"Why don't you paint me, then? I see you got a big imagination. Immortalize me on canvas."

He gave me a strange look with a half smile.

"What?" I laughed.

"I already painted you on my iPad," he said just above a whisper.

He thought I didn't hear him, but I did. I laughed on the inside because he had to be really watching me to draw me on the iPad.

"What did you say?" I asked for clarity.

Zyrese didn't say anything. He grabbed my hand and walked me over to his sofa. That was about the only thing that wasn't painted on. He then picked up his iPad and sat next to me before using facial recognition to open it. He slid over a few pictures before turning it to face me.

I wanted to cry. I couldn't believe he had drawn me on his device. It was an off-guard picture of me standing by the tree, smiling with my head down on the phone. I felt myself blushing. I didn't even remember what I was looking at on my phone that day.

"How did you? When did you?" was all I could ask because I was flabbergasted. Every detail was to perfection. The only thing missing was color. I ran my hand over my features, and they were so lifelike.

"I gotta download an app to add color, but I want to paint you on canvas when the day comes," he said, and I felt goosebumps cover my arms.

I wanted to tell him everything that was going on, but it wasn't the right time. I didn't want to do what my father asked, but I didn't have a choice because my education was on the line. I passed him back the iPad and put my head down. It was quiet for a few seconds before he spoke.

"Who called you earlier in your room? Your entire vibe changed, and it ain't been the same since. What's up?" he asked me.

I grabbed his hand because I knew I couldn't give him the truth, but I hated to lie.

"That was my father, and I didn't like the shit he was telling me, so I listened to him talk before he disconnected the call." That was all the truth that I could give him.

I needed to get away from him because I knew my feelings for him would fuck up what I was trying to do. Ironically, while I was trying to make him fall in love with me, I was falling in love with him. I wanted it to be genuine and true, not forced and under obligations and stipulations.

"I gotta go, Zyrese, but I'll see you tomorrow," I told him as I stood to my feet.

He stood with me and begged to walk me to the door. He stopped before opening it.

"You promise?" he asked, holding out his pinky finger.

I smiled and locked my pinky with his. This was going to be the hardest shit I had to do because when the dust settled, both of our hearts would get broken. He leaned over to kiss my cheek, and I felt bubbly inside. I could tell he didn't fuck with too many people because outside of Trahan's rude ass, I didn't see him with other people, especially females.

"Don't make promises that you can't keep, Jadior. I already know too much about that shit," he said with a little bass in his voice. I wanted to drag him to the sofa, put my feet under me, and pry whatever caused him to feel that way out of him, but my mind knew he wouldn't tell me. I knew he didn't trust easily, so it would take some time to pull back some of his layers.

"I would never break a promise because I like you. Promises have been broken in my life as well." I thought about my parents trying to avenge my sister's death from years ago and dangling my life in front of me for it.

Zyrese stood back and looked at me. I felt like he could see through me, and I didn't need that. I quickly hugged him, but when I tried to let go, he held onto me tighter.

"I know whatever this shit is, it's new, and we don't know where it's going, but whatever this is, don't lie to me, and don't break my heart," he said before letting me go.

I gave him one last look before leaving his apartment and walking back to my room. He didn't ask to walk with me, and I was glad because I couldn't bear to be around him any longer, knowing what I was sent to do.

CHAPTER SIX

MAGNOLIA

After Zyrese left, I pulled my Xanax and two fentanyl pills out of my back pocket and threw them bitches back. I didn't feel like hearing their fucking mouths because they didn't know what the fuck I was going through mentally. Of course, my wife and I had our fights and arguments, but we never separated. The shit felt strange, and I couldn't handle being away from her. No communication. I couldn't pick up my fucking phone and call her. I couldn't touch her. I couldn't go to where she was and drag her ass home.

I had to be strategic about shit and think smarter than those Haitian niggas because I knew how they got down. Right now, I had to figure out what the fuck was going on and why the fuck Kadafi set me up with this crazy ass nigga. And what the fuck did that nurse mean when she told me to ask my fucking brother about my wife. Either I was paranoid, or my potnah and my fucking brother were plotting on me. I didn't want to think the worst, but I didn't trust nobody but Zenobia at this point.

I stood in front of the door for a minute until I felt the pills take effect. I let the cool air hit my face to keep me calm because I wanted to go in there and air them motherfuckers out, but I knew that was my paranoia getting the best of me, and I couldn't let it. Tingling in my arms. Eyes getting low. Everything moving in slow motion, from the trees to the plants that lined my driveway. I rubbed my beard because I knew the pills had kicked in along with the shots I had taken, and I would function better.

I turned to walk in the door and stumbled a little because it had been a while since I had taken pills. I knew Zenobia would be mad at me if she knew what the fuck I was doing, but she wasn't here to be a nigga's medicine. My mind was fucked up, and all those niggas could get hot lead pumped in them if their answers didn't align, brother or not. I closed the door slowly and felt myself getting dizzy, but I shook it off. I walked back to the room where everybody was, and they all looked at me.

"What the fuck did you take?" Jahari was the first one to notice, but I wouldn't give him the answer that he was looking for because I was grown and didn't answer to anyone other than God and my wife.

I swaggered over to them, not paying his dumb ass any attention, and went back to where my gun was. I was the one asking the questions. My eyes landed on Kadafi.

"Imma ask you like I asked these other niggas. Do you want your wife to hear or see what the fuck we about to talk about?" I asked him, and he cocked his head to the side.

Makesa looked innocent and submissive, so I knew if he told her ass to leave the room, she would go willingly.

"Nah, she can stay with me. She's really not a people person. What all this shit about anyway?" Kadafi spoke. "And why you got that big ass gun sitting on the counter? You plan on killing one of us?" He laughed like shit was funny

"If time permits, and I don't get the right fucking answers," I told him with a straight face.

"I'm 'bout to call Momma because yo' ass tripping, nigga," Jahari said like a lil bitch.

When he pulled his phone out of his pocket, I yanked that bitch and sent it crashing to the floor. I knew he wasn't gon' buck because I was the big brother, and I prayed Amerika didn't get involved in men's business and felt froggy because I would clothesline the fuck out of her.

"The fuck wrong with you, nigga? You got us all over here and breaking shit and ain't said nothing. You know Mhyesha could get that noise out yo' ass, but you ain't have to break my fucking phone," he whined like a bitch.

Amerika just rolled her eyes at me because she was crazy, but she knew to stay in her place when shit got real.

"Okay, bruh, you made your point. What's going on, and where is Zenobia? You are high, and you're losing it," Khaza said, standing up. He ain't have shit to do with this. He was here by default.

I came from around the corner with the rifle in my hand and stood in the middle of them. My eyes locked with my brother and Kadafi. They were standing side by side.

"I chose a care team to take care of my fucking son when he was bought home to this fucking house. I even had the best guards on my team keeping an eye on him while I handled business," I said, looking at Kadafi.

"I asked you was this nigga Khap straight because I wanted a smooth transition back to the streets with no bullshit. Hand him the fucking money, and my shipments of fucking guns would be at the port in Florida, right?" I asked.

"Nigga, what the fuck are you talking about? Khap is crazy, but when it comes to the fucking money, he gon' chase it. He ain't give me no static when I asked him to fuck with you. He said long as you had the fucking money, then everything was good, so what the fuck you talking about?" Kadafi had stepped in my face, pushing his wife behind him.

I scratched my chin and looked into his eyes for a few seconds longer than I should have. His pupils didn't shift from side to side, so I knew he was telling the truth. We backed up slowly from the other, and I was back in the center of everybody. My eyes met Jahari's. I scratched my head because the dizziness was getting heavy.

"Nigga, what you took?" he asked me, and I looked at him.

"Fuck what I took nigga. You got some answers that I need out yo' fucking throat?" My words were a little slurred, but I didn't give a fuck. My head started to spin, but I shook that shit off. He looked at me, confused.

"The fuck are you talking about, nigga?" He was trying to play dumb like he didn't remember what the fuck he told me. I started piecing shit together, and now the shit was starting to make perfect sense.

"Remember on New Year's Eve when you, Mhyesha, and I were sitting at the table talking. You were telling us about how Amerika burned the fucking house down because she walked in on you fucking a bitch doggystyle?" I asked.

I knew she was embarrassed, but she wanted to stay for the fucking shit show, so she would catch the shit.

"The bitch that died in that fire was that nigga's sister, and now my fucking wife is over there going through God knows what because you decided to cheat on your fucking wife with a Haitian bitch," I told him, and it was his turn to look stupid. He was processing what the fuck I was saying, and Amerika's mouth dropped to the fucking floor.

"The fuck? Just tell all my fucking business, nigga." Jahari came toward me, and I upped my rifle.

"Nigga, back the fuck up. Yo' wife is beside you. Mine isn't, and it's because of you. I ain't trying to explain to Mhyesha the reason I killed my fucking brother," I told him, but he didn't move.

"I'm so sorry, Magnolia. I didn't know what was going on." That was Amerika, but she didn't have shit to be sorry about.

"Nah, luv, this ain't on you. You did what any fucking wife would have done in that situation. That's this nigga's fault for sticking his dick where it didn't belong. How the fuck did y'all meet, anyway, all the way in California? I'm curious," I told him, standing my gun beside me and folding my arms. I had to hear this fucking story. "How long were y'all fucking before you brought her home?" I was being sarcastic, and he knew it because he rolled his eyes.

"I had been fucking with her for a year and some change because she was gonna get me the connect with some Haitian ingredients to enhance our weed. I offered her money, but she wanted me. I was fucked up when she found out where I lived, and she caught me on a drunk night when Amerika was out of town," he explained.

I saw the tears rolling down Amerika's cheeks. Makeda went over to hug her.

"Nigga, you make your own fucking weed. The fuck you need they shit for? What if that bitch was giving you some voodoo shit that made motherfuckers crazy. Did you ever fucking think about that? Did you ever stop to think that shit was a fucking setup?" I told him, and he hung his head low.

"Is that why you didn't want to fucking tell me everything, Jahari? Because you were doing shit behind my back?" Amerika walked up to him.

I was too high to even get in between them. Plus, she needed to get in his ass.

"Amerika, it wasn't like that." He tried to hold her hands, but he couldn't.

Whap, whap, whap, whap.

That sound rang through the house as she smacked his cheek from left to right. They weren't love taps either. She was fucking his face up. No scratches, all licks. He was trying to block them, but he couldn't because she was too fast. That shit made me think about my wife and how she would put her fucking hands on me, and I would take it because I knew I had fucked up, but not like he had. He went against the code. We all have fucking cheated, but to bring a bitch to your house is the ultimate betrayal. Amerika was strong as fuck because I knew Zenobia would have left me and fucked up everything we owned, and I would have killed the entire world until it was just us left. He was eating those licks, but that shit was enough because we had bigger fish to fry.

"Answer your wife, nigga. She deserves that fucking much," I told him, and he cut his eyes at me. "Take your wife in one of the many fucking rooms we got in this bitch and fix it because this shit is your fault," I told him.

I watched as he went to grab her, and she started to swing on him again. This time, he lifted her up and threw her over his shoulder with her yelling and screaming, kicking and punching his back as he took her to the back of the house.

"Nigga, you trying to kill everybody, but we got more pressing shit to be concerned about. How the fuck we gon' get Zenobia back, and you can't even talk to her? You don't know what the fuck they doing to her over there. I say we gather our army and go in guns blazing," Khaza said, stepping to me.

This crazy ass nigga was down for whatever, and I liked that about him, but we couldn't do that. I didn't want to risk my wife getting hurt behind me running in there on some rowdy shit.

"Nah, Khap ain't like that. He don't move like that. I understand why he doing the shit, but he ain't gon hurt her," Kadafi said like that made shit any better.

"Why the fuck he wants my wife, though? I didn't kill his sister." I had to ask.

"It's bigger than that shit because niggas like him know about the life they live, and she was just a casualty for being in the United States, trying to start her own business without the family. I been knowing they family for years, and one thing they don't do is hurt females, so I know he ain't gon' hurt her. Plus, that nigga married, and I know he don't wanna play that fucking game. I may have known his family for years, but you like a fucking brother to me, Magnolia. Whatever move you wanna go with, you know I'm fucking with it, but those pills gotta fucking go, bruh. I need you with a straight head," Kadafi told me, but I wasn't trying to hear that shit.

I wanted my wife, and they didn't understand because they had their wives.

"I get it, nigga. You miss your wife, but the oils not gon solve shit. You need your head on a swivel because don't you have some Chinese niggas behind you, too?" he asked me, and I wondered how he knew that shit.

"Nigga, don't nothing fly past me because I know everything. I told you, you my fucking brother. Blood couldn't make us any closer, but Jahari in his feelings, and that's his fuck up that he gotta fix with his fucking wife. We gotta get Zenobia back. A war may start, but we gon come back with the fucking victory because what is every nigga's weakness?" he asked me, and we all made eye contact.

"Pussy," we all said in unison, but I wasn't trying to take that nigga wife, I just wanted mine back. I would go to war for my wife, but I wasn't on no kidnapping shit. I would kill that nigga first.

"Well, we got little time to put a plan together, so no one

gets hurt and to get shit situated before making our move, but we only got this once chance, nigga. We gon' be moving in another country where they don't mind dying.

I didn't give a fuck what any of them was saying. My eyes locked with Khaza, and he already knew what the fuck was up. I didn't mind dying if that meant my wife and kids could live because I was dying inside without her. I would plant a fucking bomb on each corner of Haiti to get my wife, and we could watch that motherfucker go up in flames because that's how I moved. Fuck him and his family because I was trying to do business with the nigga, but he had ulterior motives.

"Nigga, whatever you thinking while you on that shit, you need to sleep it off because we not about to become fucking terrorists," Kadafi said as if reading my thoughts.

I walked over to him. "Don't you have your fucking wife next to you? You go to bed with her every night, right? Don't question me and what the fuck I'm thinking because you don't know my nigga. I don't need to sleep shit off because I know what the fuck I'm doing. If the situation was reversed, I know my wife would stop at fucking nothing to get to me, so Imma apply that same fucking pressure to get her back, no disrespect." I turned my head to look at Makeda, who looked scared shitless.

I knew I was overthinking because of the pills, but that was the only thing keeping me sane without Zenobia. I couldn't even think about sleep because our bed was empty on top of the shit dealing with my fucking son. Everybody grew quiet with their own thoughts, but mine was plotting to get my wife back. I heard footsteps coming down the steps and knew that it was Lexington coming to tell me something. He knew all about me killing the nurses and shit, so he had been on pins and needles giving my son around-the-clock care because he didn't want to lose his life. I turned to him, and he looked defeated. He hadn't had any sleep in days because I was paying this nigga around the clock. His face didn't look right, and I was afraid of the shit that was about to come out of his mouth.

I kept my gun close, just in case I needed it. We all turned to him because everybody present knew what the fuck was going on. His jacket was pulled off his shoulders like he had been fighting for his life. The look of sorrow was plastered on his face, and I turned my head away. I felt Kadafi, Khaza, and Bear walking closer to me like they knew something I didn't.

"The fuck y'all niggas doing?" They remained silent but kept walking toward me. The ladies and Jahari came back to the front to be there as well. I felt like a little kid getting in trouble for something that I didn't do.

"Mr. Magnolia," Lexington said in a solemn voice that I didn't care too much care for.

"Keep the Mr., it's just Magnolia. What the fuck is going on with my son?" I asked him, running out of patience. I grabbed my rifle that was leaning on my legs because I didn't know what this nigga was about to say.

"You might want to sit down because I don't know what's to come with what I am about to say to you," he told me, and I mugged him.

"I don't need to sit for what the fuck you about to tell me about my son. I trusted you to take care of him. Clearly, I couldn't trust your fucking nurses, and I killed all of them bitches because they couldn't be trusted. While you were thinking they were taking care of my fucking son, one of those bitches was killing them. I looked at the fucking footage and found out who it was, and I didn't spare none of them bitches. So, it's your job to deliver the fucking news to their families because right now, their body parts are floating in the fucking river." I could tell he was nervous because the fucking sweat drenched his face. I already knew what he was about to say before he even said it.

I never sat down. Finger tapping my gun, my niggas surrounding me, making me nervous, hands trembling, mind racing. Sweat forming on my forehead. Nauseous stomach. Leg shaking. I couldn't sit down. Too much was going on around me, and I couldn't control it. I shook that shit off and prepared my mind for what he was about to say.

"Magnolia, for the past twenty-four hours, I have been monitoring your son, and his brain has no activity. I found it strange since I was weaning him off the oxygen because his eyes had opened when you were away. I went to make coffee, and when I came back, he was coding, and the nurse was performing chest compressions. Once we got him stable, you came back and did what you had to do. I was left alone to figure out what happened when they all left.

"I checked all his IV drips and noticed a discoloration in the one linked to his heart, and I knew it was foul play. Nimodipine was injected into his bag, and that caused cardiac arrest. The shit was planned, but I knew nothing about it," he said.

I kinda believed him, but those were the bitches he chose to take care of my son. He may have had something to do with the shit, too, and was trying to spare his own life, but it was too late for that.

"I realize that he was without oxygen for more than six minutes, and that wasn't good, but I did my best to resuscitate him, and I did, but I knew the next few days were critical. Now, there is nothing else that I can do because only ten percent of his brain is functioning, and the machines are practically breathing for him. His heart is working at zero percent, and I wanted to know what you want to do," he asked like he was asking for a piece of fucking candy and not my son's fucking life.

I looked at the niggas around me, and they all looked speechless.

"Pull the plug because I'm about to snatch yours." I raised my gun and shot one to his dome. Blood and brain matter went everywhere, including all over the people around me.

"Niggaaaaa, what the fuck you killed the doctor for?" Jahari asked.

"Because he and his fucking crew killed my son. Life for a fucking life." I looked at all of them, and they said nothing but nodded their heads up and down.

"That's what the fuck I'm talking about. This the shit I live for," Khaza said, laughing.

"Shut the fuck up, Khaza. All you know is murder," Yhental said, sounding like she was about to vomit everywhere.

"Y'all help me get this nigga to my basement, so we can cut him up," I told them, and they sprang into action.

The ladies walked away because I didn't want them to help. This was a man's job.

"Nigga, I'm about to call Mhyesha because you have lost yo' fucking mind," Jahari's scary ass said as he pulled out his cell phone.

I knew he wasn't gon' help because he had a weak stomach for shit like this. I didn't care if he called my mother because the damage was done. I didn't give a fuck if Lexington had family. They would be looking for his ass for months to come, if not years.

Bear went to get the tarp to put his body on. We rolled his body onto it and picked his ass up. He was heavy for dead weight, but we managed to get him to my basement. I wasn't about to drive all the way to my slaughterhouse to cut his ass up. I had the same shit in my basement that I had there except the chains, but I didn't need them.

Khaza and I used machetes to cut his body up while Bear

made sure to drain his blood into bottles to later dispose of. After cutting his shit up, we bagged it and brought it to the awaiting black truck where one of my hittas would dispose of it. He slid me ten pills, and I put them in my pocket because I knew I would need them when I walked back into the fucking house.

We all walked in, and the women were cleaning the house to make it spotless. They didn't say anything as reality set in my fucking head. My fucking son was upstairs dead. No life lived in him anymore. I stood in the middle of the floor in my own thoughts.

"Nigga, are you okay?" I heard Bear ask me, but I couldn't answer him because I was numb.

I didn't know how I would react when I walked up those fucking stairs and saw my first-born son so fucking lifeless, lying in that bed. I didn't have my wife to be strong for me because this was a first. In the past, I didn't give a fuck who was killed or who I killed, but this shit was too close to home. My fucking son. I walked away from everybody and took the steps slowly, one by one. I heard steps behind me.

"I don't need you with me. I got this on my own."

I knew it was Jahari coming behind me, but I didn't need him trying to save me. I was the strong one, so I knew I couldn't show any type of weakness. Zenobia was the only person who could point them out, and she wasn't here, so I had to be strong because it was all I knew. I slid two pills from my pocket, swallowed them without water, and made my way up the rest of the stairs to the room. I took slow steps toward the open door because I didn't know what to expect. After saying a quick prayer, I walked fully into the fucking room with a mixture of emotions that took over me. Anger, hurt, pain, anguish, just to name a few.

As I walked closer to his bed, he looked lifeless and cold.

His skin looked clammy, like he had been dead for a while. The machines weren't on him, so Lexington knew what it was before he came downstairs. I wished I could kill that nigga again.

I walked closer to his face and ran my hand across his cheek. He was a cross between cold and warm, but I knew he was dead. There was no movement of his body. His dreads were pulled back off his face like someone had washed them. I felt tears falling down my cheeks, which I was trying to hold. I couldn't take this shit. Too much was going on around me, and I wanted to make it stop. I wanted to kill everything walking because I felt like a fucking failure. Niggas knew not to fuck with me, but I had so much fucking torture for this nigga taking my fucking son.

I fell to my knees while holding his hand and kissed it.

"God, I prayed that I would never have to bury any of my kids, and this happened. What did I do to deserve this? I changed my ways, and that still wasn't enough. I need answers, please!" I yelled loud as fuck and didn't care who heard me. I was on my knees for a good few minutes before I stood and straightened my posture. Those were the last tears I would cry because it was war moving forward.

"I called Mhyesha. I didn't tell her what was going on, but I told her she needed to get here asap and leave the kids with Gianni." Jahari came up behind me, and I didn't even hear him.

I knew Daisy loved MJ, so it was only right that she knew what the fuck was going on, but I didn't want to be the one to tell her. I'd let Amerika do the honors because I wasn't in the right headspace to tell anybody anything.

CHAPTER SEVEN
MHYESHA

"Boy, if you don't stop that fucking crying, Imma give you something to cry for," I kept telling Mason because, for the past few days, he had been crying for any little thing.

When he wanted something to drink, he whined when he asked me. I knew something was wrong because the shit started a few days ago. Mason never cried when he came by his Gigi because we always had fun.

"Gigi, he just crying because he wanna go home," Monae's sassy ass said as she finished polishing my nails. I loved having my grandbabies because they were a reflection of my son.

"Girl, hush. He loves being by Gigi because he can do whatever he wants, huh Mason?" I asked him as he walked to me and squeezed his way between my legs to sit on my lap.

Gianni was in the kitchen making homemade pizza and wings because we were about to have a movie day. I knew Magnolia would call for his kids because he was overprotective when it came to them, but I understood because I was like that when it came to my boys. I was surprised he hadn't called yet for me to bring them home. Jonae was polishing my other hand, but she was so quiet. She was my good Gigi baby. Very polite and obedient, but Monae was Project Pat. Always had some shit to say when she wasn't being spoken to. I didn't tell her anything because she was a child and didn't know better. Long as she didn't cuss, I would stay off her ass.

"Monae, it's just five fingers. What the hell taking you so long to polish them?"

Jonae had already finished my other hand and had them drying under the fan.

"Perfection takes time, Gigi. I'm almost finished." She had the nerve to roll her eyes at me.

All I could do was laugh because she didn't know shit from sugar. She put a topcoat on my pinky, then slid my hand by the fan as Mason crawled on my lap and laid his head on my chest. He was being overly affectionate. He was usually under me, but this was overdoing it. I knew some shit was up, but I couldn't put my finger on it. I hoped everything was okay in Georgia, but that's where my thoughts were leading.

"What's up with lil man?" Gianni walked into the living room, where I had made it into a mini hair salon. There was nothing I wouldn't do for my grandbabies.

"I don't know, but something is going on. He don't usually be like this. I know a lot is going on in Georgia. He might be missing his Mommy," I told him as he sat next to me.

"Have you talked to Nobby or Magnolia lately? One of them would usually call to check on the kids?" he asked.

"No, and that's what's bothering me a little," I told him, and he reached over to kiss my cheek.

"Then try not to worry because if something was wrong, they would call. So, stop overthinking, and let's enjoy our grandkids."

That put a smile on my face because he said *our*.

I didn't think about being with another man after Mason was killed until I met Gianni. I knew he worked closely with my son, but I had been watching him for years. I looked good for my age, but I also knew he probably wanted kids because he was so young. I watched from the sidelines as he handled business and laid niggas down, and it turned me on. It wasn't until he approached me that I knew he felt the same way I did.

We were at a family gathering, and I was sitting alone at the table. Everybody was minding their own business, but he couldn't keep his eyes off me and vice versa. When he came around, he would never get too close to me because Magnolia watched everything. He would steal little glances at me, and I would blush like a schoolgirl. When Magnolia met Nobby, all bets were off. His attention was focused on her, and that worked in my favor.

I was sitting at the table by myself, on my phone, and Gianni walked up with a glass of champagne in his hand.

"You look lonely over here by yourself," he said and handed me my glass.

"I may be alone, but I'm never lonely." I tapped my purse, and he got the hint.

"Oh, you rolling like that?" he asked.

"Do you see who my son is? I have to roll like this because he is a livewire.

"Of course I do, but just know I got him," he said, and that shit turned me on. Big Mason never said that about any of our sons. "I always have my nigga's back, even when he's not paying attention," he continued, and I blushed because that meant he was a protector.

"But enough about yo' son because he good." He nodded. We both looked in Magnolia's direction, and he was all in Nobby's ass.

"I want you, though. I'm trying to see what's up with you," he told me, and I almost spit out my drink.

"My son would kill me if I fucked with his right-hand man, and

I'm old enough to be your fucking momma, boy. You better stop," I told him, and he laughed.

"Age ain't nothing but a number. The ball is in my court, and don't no nigga run my life. I love Magnolia, but I got a life outside this shit, and it's about to be you, so what's up?" He was aggressive, and I loved it. I guess I was taking too long to answer him because he grabbed my hand, and I stood from my seat. He led me to a corner where no one could see. Then, he took my drink from my hand and set it on the table. He backed me against the wall, and I looked around, breathing heavily.

"What you scared for? You are safest with me because I would kill any nigga who brought you any harm, including your son," he said.

I knew he was tripping because my son was a monsta.

He moved against my body, pressing me into the brick wall behind us, inches away from my lips.

"See how easy it was for me to get you alone? Who paying attention? You ain't gotta look around because I got you." He was so close to my lips that they were almost touching.

"That pussy wet, huh? I know it's fat. You gon' let me touch her?"

Before I could reply, his hand slipped up the front of my dress but was met with hard steel.

"Oh, you too, huh?" he whispered against my lips.

"Can't leave one without the other," I told him, and he bypassed the gun I had strapped to my leg.

I didn't have panties on, and my pussy was soaked. His middle finger slid into my slit, and I could hear the sounds as he slid his thumb to circle my clit.

"I knew you was fucking with me, but you playing hard or you scared, but you don't have to be," he told me, and my hand slid down to his dick.

I jumped because his girth scared me.

"Don't jump. That's how you make a nigga feel every time I see you and can't touch you. So, this shit right here is chef's kiss." His finger moved in a circle, and I began to moan.

"I know a nigga ain't touched you since big Mason."

He told the truth, so I couldn't argue. My hands went to his chest.

"Please." I bit my bottom lip.

"Nah, fuck that begging shit. This shit was destined to happen." He sucked in my bottom lip.

"I know you have women your age who would die to be where I am right now, so why you fucking with me?" I asked him.

He chuckled, sucking my top lip.

"Fuck them. I want you. Can't nobody take your place if I put you there, so stop beating around the bush and tell me what you want, Mhyesha." He was driving me crazy with his breath tickling my face. He used his other hand to pull my dress over my ass and lifted me in the air. I heard him fumbling with his belt, and I didn't stop him.

"I can't give you kids, Gianni!" I blurted out, trying to get him off me.

"Fuck them kids. Your sons gon' give us grandkids because you gon' be my wife."

I wrapped my arms around his neck and my legs around his waist.

"Good girl." I looked down and saw how big his dick was and shook.

"I promise Imma take you slow. Just hold on for the ride," he told me and licked his fingers that had my juices on them.

I felt the tip of his dick at the tip of my opening, and he reached between us to rub his head up and down my opening.

"She so sloppy for me. Yeah, you gon' be my wife," he said as he inserted his dick inch by inch inside me.

We rocked and rolled in that corner until the party was over, and I heard someone call my name. By then, we were done, and he was helping me pull my dress back down, and I helped him get his belt and shit together. Before we walked back out, he grabbed my chin, kissing my lips and whispering.

"Be ready to tell yo' son you about to be Mrs. Gianni. I got shit on my end," he said and swaggered away from me.

I smiled at the thought because he meant he was gon' marry me, and he did. I fell in love with him that day at the party in the small corner, with him making love to the pussy. He didn't even know that, but it didn't matter at this point because it was us against the world since we made shit official, and that was years ago.

"What are you over there smiling about?"

I didn't even know I was smiling. I looked over at him, blushing because he still looked the same way he looked when we got married. He hadn't changed at all.

"You and that shit at the party," I told him honestly.

"All those years ago." He shook his head. "Did I not make good on my promise? I told you what I wanted and made it happen with no problems.

"You did, and I couldn't be happier that you chose me, with my old ass," I told him, laughing.

"Nah, not old, just seasoned very well."

I blushed because he always made me feel like a fucking woman. So feminine and sexy, even at my age. I knew he could have any woman he wanted, but he said he needed me, and I felt that shit with my entire being. We been locked in ever since. Magnolia gave us static at first, but when I dug into his ass because Nobby was way younger than him, he shut the fuck up and let me live my life. He told Gianni he would smoke him if he hurt me, and Gianni laughed because he didn't have any plans to hurt me.

"That's right, baby," I told him and reached over with

Mason's long, big ass on my body to kiss him. He still hadn't fallen asleep. I took my hands away from the fan to feel his head to make sure that he didn't have a fever because he was being too clingy.

"You think he's sick?" Gianni asked.

"No, I just think he misses his parents. He's feeling some shit and wants to be near them, that's all," I told him.

I went to pick him up off my chest, but he hugged me tighter, so I let him. If he wanted me to hold him all day, I would so he could be peaceful.

I knew something was going on, but I didn't know if it was good or bad. When kids felt some shit going on with their parents, they were silent and clingy with the person they felt the safest with. For Mason, it was me, and I understood it.

"You think we should call them?" he asked.

"Nah, if something was going on, I know they would call me. I took the kids so they could take care of their affairs before I bought them back home. They needed this break," I told my husband because he was starting to worry. His street senses started to kick in, but I needed him to be my husband.

Magnolia must have thought I didn't know what the fuck was going on. I knew all of them niggas were out there handling business. I knew all about him working with those Haitians in the gun trade. The shit was tricky, but I knew he could handle shit. He had his niggas, but I had some not too far behind. I knew he went to Haiti, but that was the last I heard because I pulled my soldiers away from that shit. Them niggas were crazy over there, and I wasn't about to risk their lives because they had families to live for.

I had old-school hittas and snipers, so it was nothing to make a phone call and see what the fuck was going on, but I trusted my son to make the right moves. He wasn't a dummy and knew what the fuck he was doing. That piece of information I kept, and I hated to keep secrets from my husband, but this shit here was for the best because I needed him with me. The first thing he would have done was talk Magnolia out of going, and he wouldn't have listened, so that was a conversation that didn't need to be had between me and my husband.

We didn't need any static between us because if Gianni knew that Magnolia was going to Haiti, he would have been on the first thing smoking with him out there, and I would have had to physically fight with him not to go. He dabbled every now and then, but for the most part, he was my husband first.

I stood to my feet because Mason had finally fallen asleep, and I went to put him in bed. Monae and Jonae were in their room playing with their iPads or whatever they had, and the pizza was in the oven. I needed affection from my husband because my heart was heavy for some reason, and I knew he felt that shit too. After laying Mason in the bed, I walked back to the living room, and he had already put everything up. I didn't want to go to the bedroom, and I knew the twins wouldn't come out for hours because they had their own refrigerator filled to the brim with everything they needed, so we had a good five hours to play.

Gianni was sitting on the sofa, lighting his blunt with his legs cocked open. I could see his dick print as he opened then closed his legs. My mouth watered as I walked over to him. I had on my silk gown with spaghetti straps because the twins and I were having a spa day. I didn't have panties on because I didn't like them, and this pussy needed to breathe. I didn't allow him to smoke around the kids, so he had been going on the porch, but they were in the room, so we were good. I walked between his legs and looked down at him. My husband was sexy as fuck, and we complimented each other very well. With the blunt dangling from his mocha lips, he leaned up and caressed from my legs to my hips.

"No panties, huh?" he asked with a raised brow.

"You know I don't ever wear them," I told him.

"You tryna smoke with yo' husband?" he asked.

I straddled him, landing directly on his hard dick. I spread my thighs so he could feel my wetness through his sweats. I took the blunt from his hand and put it to my mouth. Gianni grabbed my waist, putting his mouth to mine. He wanted a shotgun, so he opened his mouth, connecting his lips with mine while I inhaled, and then blew the smoke into his mouth. It always intensified my high. I felt my eyes getting low, and my body tingled. My clit thumped against his dick, and he felt it. He made his dick jump, and I bit my bottom lip.

"You like that shit, huh?" He groaned and reached under me to pull his dick out.

I lifted a little and sat down on it. No need to ease it in because I was already leaking like a faucet. I didn't move my hips or rock and forth; I just sat there. I needed to feel this shit. He thumped inside me, and my clit was on fire. I gave him the blunt back, and he put it in the ashtray and gripped my ass cheeks to get deeper. I opened my thighs wider for him to get deeper. This shit felt heavenly. I could sit like this forever, but I knew I couldn't. All the shit was just a distraction from the way my heart beat rapidly, but I couldn't figure out why. I began to move a little, but he stopped me. He grabbed each side of my face and looked into my eyes.

"What's wrong, bae? This ain't you. I love the pussy, you know that, but something is weighing heavy on you, and what type of fucking husband would I be if I didn't pay attention to the love of my life? My wife." He moaned because I knew my pussy was tight and warm.

"Whatever it is, you and I know I can fix it, so what's up?"

I didn't want to talk about that shit. I just wanted some dick and to lie down before my babies got up for movie night. I tried to kiss his neck, but he kept my face up because he knew I was trying to distract him.

"If you don't tell me what the fuck is going on, Imma throw this good ass pussy off me and let myself get blue balls because we don't keep fucking secrets, Mhyesha, so what the fuck is up?" he asked again, and I ignored his ass again.

I rotated my hips in a circle. He tried to switch his hands from my face to my hips, but it was too deep. I already had his ass hypnotized, and he couldn't control it. He gripped my hips, guiding me back and forth, up and down, making sure his dick grazed my clit with every movement.

"You better not make a fucking sound," he said, grabbing the front of my neck with one hand and my hip with the other.

Gianni was fucking me back slow and hard, driving me crazy. He knew what the fuck he was doing; he wanted to rush the shit, so we could talk, but I had a trick for his ass. When I got done with him, he would forget about everything we were supposed to be talking about. I tried to keep control but was fighting a losing battle because his ass was strong.

"I ain't forget, bae," he moaned, and I couldn't answer because the dick was in my stomach.

All I could do was let my head fall back because the shit was feeling too good.

"You don't forget nothing, Gianni, but this dick got me forgetting everything." I moaned.

"Didn't I tell you not to make a sound until I told yo' ass to? I see you wanna be a bad girl, huh?" He let go of my hips and stood to his feet, stepping out of his joggers.

His legs were pure muscle. I held onto his neck as his hand met my hips and controlled the rhythm. Up, down, circle, up, down, circle was the rhythm. We were so into fucking each other's brains out that I didn't hear my phone ringing.

"That's yo' phone, bae. You wanna answer it?" I shook my head up and down.

Without losing the rhythm, he walked us into the kitchen, where my phone was. He sat me on the countertop and handed me my phone. As he slow stroked me, I noticed it was Jahari calling me.

"What, boy? I'm fucking my husband. What Amerika done to yo' ass now?" I swear my boys never grew up.

"Mommy..." he hadn't called me mommy since he was a child. I knew something was fucking wrong.

"What's wrong, Jahari?" My voice was shaky, and Gianni had stopped moving.

"You gotta get to Georgia now and leave the kids because they don't need to see this shit," he said and disconnected the call.

I pushed Gianni away from me and hopped off the counter.

"Call Cynthia and ask her to come over and keep the kids. Some shit ain't right, and we gotta take the jet to Magnolia in Georgia," I told Gianni, and he sprang into action.

I took a quick shower, threw on a jumpsuit, and we were out the door as soon as Cynthia came because I needed to know what the fuck was going on with my fucking children. I got up to check on Mason, and he was still sleeping. Gianni got the pizza out of the oven and set it on the counter so Cynthia could see it. I didn't give a fuck about packing no bag or none of that shit. When Jahari's tone of voice changed, I knew I had to go quick. I knew what it looked like when he lost control and nobody was safe. I walked back to the living room, and my husband was standing there, matching my fly. I grabbed my phone and called to make sure the jet was fueled.

"I called a car to come get us. They should be outside in a minute," Gianni said, and I felt like I was in the twilight zone.

My hands trembled. Mind racing. All types of shit going

through my skull as I thought about what could have happened. Why the fuck was Jahari in Georgia, and why didn't Nobby fucking call me? Shit wasn't adding up, and I couldn't understand why. I stared off in a daze because I felt like I couldn't steady my pace.

"Mhyesha, let's go." He snapped me out of my zone and grabbed my hand before we walked out the door.

I didn't even remember grabbing my keys or putting on my shoes. I looked down at my feet.

"I put them on for you because you couldn't. You were shaking too bad, and I knew you couldn't do it. I got your purse and phone right here," he said as he opened the back door to the black-on-black Escalade for me to get in.

The strip wasn't far from the house, but I knew it would be far for me because I was trying to wrap my mind around what the fuck could be going on that they couldn't call me first.

"Stop wrecking yo' brain. I'm sure it's serious but not detrimental. Ain't nothing we can't fix. You know how we move." I knew he was talking about violence, but I had a feeling in my gut that it wasn't about that. The shit was on a deeper level.

I was a strong woman but weak for my boys. They were my weakness. Anything they went through, I felt that shit in my soul. Gianni held my hand the entire ride to the strip, gripping it every so often along the way. He knew how I felt on the inside because he knew I would move the earth for my sons.

"I can't help it, Gianni. They didn't call me first, and I don't understand that. They know I would set the world on fire for them, and it angers me that I feel like I'm the last one they called." I was being honest because that shit hurt.

"You ever thought they could handle the shit themselves and didn't want to bother you with it? Don't think of yourself as a last resort. They are grown men, and they were trying to handle it themselves. It probably got out of hand, and Jahari had to call you because you know Magnolia wasn't," he said, and it made sense.

Magnolia was always a protector, and his pride could sometimes hinder him from doing what's right. He got that shit from his father, but they were nothing alike.

"I don't give a fuck about none of that shit. He should have called me. If he could call Jahari and have his ass fly all the fucking way from California, and I was the closest, in New Orleans."

Gianni didn't fucking understand what the fuck I was talking about. He was making me mad because he knew Magnolia just like I did. He had been working alongside him for years.

"I know you don't give a fuck, but I'm letting yo' smart mouth ass know that whatever it is, we gon' work the shit out as a family." His tone remained even. It didn't matter how rowdy I got with him; he always remained humble, and I loved that about him.

We finally made it to the strip, and like the gentleman he was, he got out and came around to open the door for me. We walked to the strip hand in hand and got on the jet. Instead of sitting next to me, Gianni sat across from me. I didn't say anything because my mind was on my kids and what the fuck was going on. I fastened my seatbelt, getting ready for take-off, and he did the same. A bottle of champagne was brought out with flutes. I knew he wasn't gon' to drink, but I needed it. I filled my glass to the rim as I watched him roll a gar for us to smoke. The luxury of having a private jet.

Gianni pulled a lighter from his pocket and lit the blunt. He inhaled, then exhaled a few times before handing it to me. I inhaled the smoke into my lungs and exhaled, letting everything in my mind go. I felt mellow and okay with everything, but I knew once this bitch landed, my anxiety would return until I knew what the fuck was going on. I felt my eyes get low, and I was sure they were red as I looked at Gianni. He had his hair in a messy bun, and his skin was beautiful. I had to focus on him to forget shit and believe that he could handle whatever was happening.

"Why you looking at a nigga like that?" he asked, licking his juicy lips.

"How am I looking at you?" I replied with my thighs opening and closing.

"Like you need yo' husband to relieve some of your stress. Is that true?" he asked, and I didn't say anything.

My husband knew what time it was when I was under stress. He hit the blunt before putting it out in the ashtray. His low eyes made me melt every time. Eye contact was the shit with my husband because it was like he could read my thoughts. We were high in the air, so it was safe to take off the seatbelts. He released his belt and stood to his feet. It wasn't that much space between us, so he reached his long body over and released mine as well. We never broke eye contact as he kneeled before me. His hands went to my feet to slide off my shoes and push them to the side. He slid his hands along each side of my hips until he got to the rim of my pants.

"Lift up."

I lifted my ass a little for him to fully pull my pants down because a bitch didn't have time for panties. I never wore them, and he knew it. He pulled my pants all the way to my ankles and folded them. Then, he placed them neatly on the side of me in the seat and looked back at me. He rubbed up and down my thighs, licking his lips and looking at me. My clit thumped because I knew he was about to devour me. His hands rubbed the inside of my thighs, and my head fell back in agony.

"You gon' let me eat?" He continued to massage my legs, slowly opening them.

I relaxed my muscles as he dipped lower between my thighs. The cool breeze against my clit made the sensation intensify. I spread my thighs wider, linking my legs in the arms of the seat to give him a better view.

"She leaking and ready for me, just how I like her. She dripping on the seat, and you know I hate to waste a good meal." He moaned, his hand rubbing my clit.

I rotated my hips to meet his finger. I knew I was about to nut, but he stopped. His entire face attacked my pussy, and I was shook. I rocked and rolled my hips against his mouth as he ate my shit off the bone. My body vibrated as his tongue entered my hole. He was tongue fucking me while his thumb strummed my clit, driving me insane. He knew I couldn't take the combination. Sweat formed on the top of my lip as I let go and grabbed his head, pulling the rubber band that held his hair together. He loved when I massaged his head while he gave me head. It was our aphrodisiac.

His tongue moved like thunder across my pussy, and I couldn't control it. Up, down, asshole to clit, circles. His mouth was vicious. He grabbed my hips to stop my movements but kept eating. I gripped his hair tighter, and his tongue went faster.

"Ohhh, fuck, I'm about to nut," I moaned loud as fuck.

I didn't give a damn who heard me. The entire United States could hear me moaning.

"I know. Let that shit flow in my mouth," he said between licks.

A cool sensation went through my body as I released everything I had inside me.

"Damn, you squirted all in a nigga's eye and shit." He tapped my thigh as he stood to his feet.

I shook my head, laughing because he made a joke out of everything. He reached into the console and grabbed the wipes to clean me because I couldn't move. My legs were numb. I jumped every time the wipe touched my clit because it was extra sensitive. He picked my legs up and closed them before reaching over to grab my pants.

"I know you gotta piss, but Imma put yo' pants on first. I don't need nobody seeing all my ass."

I stood and stepped into my pants as he smacked my ass cheeks. He was so possessive. He pulled my pants up around my waist and helped me into my shoes. I walked off to go to the bathroom because I knew we were about to land soon. By airplane, we were just an hour and a half away. Gianni walked behind me to the bathroom. We both couldn't fit, but I knew he wanted to clean his face, so we crammed inside together. While he cleaned his face and beard, I pissed.

We walked back to our seats, but this time, he didn't sit across from me but beside me. We put our seat belts on and prepared for landing. While he finished smoking his blunt, I laid my head on his shoulder and rubbed his hair with a heavy heart because I didn't know what the fuck I was walking into.

When the flight landed, a car was there to get us, and they already knew where we were going. The closer we got, the faster my heart raced. It took us about thirty minutes before we pulled up to the house. Something felt off. It was eerily quiet, and that was a good thing. The last time we were here wasn't that good, but today, it was totally different. It felt like when I walked into that house, my life as I knew it would change forever. I didn't like that feeling. The last time I had that type of feeling was when Big Mason died. I was crushed, but I got over it. This wasn't the same. I knew in my heart that shit was about to change, and not for the fucking better.

Before the car could come to a complete stop, I opened the

door and hopped out. I didn't want Gianni to stop me because he couldn't. I needed to see what the fuck was going on, and waiting for Gianni to come around wasn't it. I bolted to the door. Not bothering to knock, I twisted the doorknob and rushed in. I didn't see anybody at first.

"Jahari, Magnolia," I yelled at the top of my lungs.

For a few minutes, no one answered, and then Jahari came in with a sad and defeated look on his face. Behind him were Khaza, Bear, Endymion, and, I want to say, Kadafi. I hadn't seen his ass in so long, so I knew it wasn't fucking good. Their wives followed them out, but nobody said anything. They had their heads down like the fuck they were in a cult. I looked at all of them and realized Magolia was missing, but someone else was missing, too.

"Where the fuck is Magnolia and Zenobia?" They knew I was serious because I rarely used the girl's real name.

"Magnolia is upstairs, but Zenobia was kidnapped in Haiti," was all I heard before I ran upstairs.

The shit wasn't registering in my head because why the fuck was Nobby kidnapped in Haiti? And why was Magnolia not going to fucking get her? I turned to look at everybody in the fucking room before proceeding upstairs to check on my other son, who was probably losing his shit.

"Y'all motherfuckers better figure out how to get my daughter-in-law back to the States, or imma fuck some shit up, and y'all don't want me to step in." I looked each of them in the eyes before I ran up the stairs to the second floor.

CHAPTER EIGHT
ZENOBIA

I was past angry. I didn't even know what to fucking think. Was that nigga high to leave me here? Bonnie and Clyde is what the fuck he was screaming, yet here I was, stuck in Haiti with motherfuckers I didn't even know. When he first left, I was in shock. He had his hittas with him who was willing to die for him, and he still left me here. It had been days since I'd heard from Magnolia, and I was pissed. This bitch Zianda was gon' make me beat the fuck out of her because all she did was stare at me every time she saw me.

I knew they had money. After Magnolia left, Khap and his wife dragged me to their Bently GT, and we drove for what felt like hours. I didn't even put up a fight, so all that extra shit his wife was doing wasn't called for. I didn't want to entertain the bitch because I loved my life too much, and I knew I was really outnumbered now. We drove for about an hour before we were in front of a white gate. The shit didn't feel like a kidnapping because, in some of the books I'd read, they had the bitches hog-tied, blindfolded, and folded like a pretzel in a trunk, but they didn't do that to me. Outside of the bitch trying to rough me up, I walked out on my own to their car and sat in the back seat untouched.

I looked up, and the house behind the gates was beautiful. It put my sit to shame. It was a replica of the White House, down to the foundation. I was in awe. Khap put his hand on the screen, and the gate opened, then he drove in. Every now and then, his wife would glance back at me with a smirk, but I kept my face straight. I didn't like this bitch, but I would never give her the satisfaction of knowing that. I looked around to see if I could escape this shit, but there were real army guards protecting this nigga like he was the president. Kadafi wasn't lying when he said this nigga damn near owned Haiti.

Khap looked at me through the mirror. "Don't ever try to escape, beautiful, because those men will slaughter you like a pig," he told me as if reading my mind.

I shifted my eyes away from his because I could give a fuck less about what he had to say.

That was days ago, and nothing had changed. I had a strange feeling in my heart that something had happened at home, but I couldn't put my finger on it. It was that motherly feeling that a woman got when she knew something was wrong with her kids. I couldn't call them, and I didn't have access to anything. They took my purse and phone the minute I got to their home.

The shit was weird. They didn't even sleep together to say they were husband and wife. The night they bought me to their home, Khap told Zianda to go to her room like she was a fucking child. Since I'd been here, I hadn't said a fucking word. My room was on the second floor, and their maids and butlers took up the first floor. Every day, they would bring my food to my room and leave it at the door because I would leave my room. The room was big as fuck. The color scheme was all black, which was creepy, but I didn't care because it wasn't mine.

I enjoyed the stay because it was a Cali king sized bed. A 65-inch television hung on the wall, and I had everything I needed in there except electronics. It was like he didn't want me to talk to anybody who could help me out of this shit. He even had a lady bring me lounge clothes and make sure I had all the toiletries I needed, so there was no need to leave the room. I hadn't seen Khap or his wife, and that was okay with me.

Over the days, I used the time to really think about some shit. My life in general. All the way back to when I first met Magnolia. I was so young and doing so fucking much that I hadn't really lived my life. Of course, I accomplished things and beat the odds because I was a doctor, but outside of that, I was just a wife and mother, and half the kids weren't even mine, but I loved them the same. I didn't get a chance to be young, wild, and free because I had Zyrese to take care of.

When my mother was killed, I had no choice but to take care of him because nobody would want a fucking kid with autism, and I wouldn't let him go to foster care. That wasn't going to happen. Then came Magnolia. He was my light at the end of the fucking tunnel. He was everything my young ass needed at the time. Everything about him, I needed. His love, ambition for me to thrive, affection, and patience with me when life became overwhelming, but was that shit really enough? Did our good really outweigh the bad?

We fought like every normal couple, but sometimes I took shit too far. I wasn't the type of woman to put my hands on my nigga unless it was out of love. Magnolia was a big nigga, and sometimes he let me fuck him up—but for good reason. The only regret I had in this life was killing my daughter. I have nightmares about that night every now and then. That led to

Magnolia needing therapy to cope, and him falling in love with the bitch, to me having to kill her. My life had been a roller-coaster from the beginning, and I was ready to get the fuck off before I lost myself.

Then, the shit with MJ was heavy on my heart. I loved that boy like I carried him for nine months, he and the twins. I accepted them with open arms because I loved their father. I missed them so much, and it hadn't even been a week. The little things we take for granted could be taken away with a snap of the fingers. That's exactly what was happening to me, and I hated it. I didn't want to talk to or see anybody, and I didn't want to be like this.

Even though my mother was a crackhead, a part of me left with her when she was killed. If it wasn't for my husband, I don't know where Zyrese and I would have ended up. Too much time to think was about to send me down a rabbit hole. Did Magnolia look at me as a charity case when we first met? My mind went to Amerika, and I knew she was probably losing her fucking mind and trying to take his head off for leaving me here. She was the one person outside of my husband who knew what I went through on a daily basis when we were younger. She always sided with Magnolia when we argued, but I knew she wanted to kill him now.

I sat in silence in the middle of the bed, letting my thoughts take over. I hadn't seen either Khap or his wife since they walked me to this room. He never told me I couldn't roam the house; I just chose not to because I wasn't familiar with anything. Plus, his wife looked like she didn't like me, so I didn't want to bump into her and beat her ass, and then they kill me. All I did was eat, shower, and cry myself to sleep every night since I had been here thinking about my family, especially my kids.

I knew they were looking for me. I knew Mhyesha was

looking for me. She treated me like I was her child. I just hoped that Magnolia didn't crash out and start popping pills again.

I heard the doorknob rattle and went to pull my shirt down. I had on a crop top with boy shorts that barely covered my ass because I knew no one would bother me, but I guess I was wrong. Half my dreads were pulled into a bun, while the rest fell because they were so long. There was still a little curl left in them, but I knew I would need a retwist soon.

The door was pushed open, and in walked Khap, dressed like he was about to go out. For the nigga to be Haitian, he dressed like a New Orleans native. Skinny Balmain jeans with the matching shirt and Js on his feet—he looked like money. His dreads hung over his shoulders, crinkled, and landing on his waist. His wrists were iced out with diamond Cuban link bracelets, while the other had an iced-out Rolex. I could even smell the Creed cologne that he wore. It went straight to my lady parts because it's the same cologne that Magnolia wore. Something was different about Khap, though. The way he carried himself was very different and slightly a turn-on. The last time I'd seen him, he had a gun in my husband's face, but now he had a totally different demeanor. I tried to pull my shirt down because I didn't have a bra on, but his words stopped me.

"You are going to rip it off trying to pull it down. It's fine, princess. You're good in here. This is your privacy," he said, walking closer to the bed.

I said nothing. I was just taking him in. I didn't have to say shit to him because I didn't want to be here. He interrupted my thoughts.

"Would you like me to get you a longer shirt?" he asked, and I rolled my eyes.

I wanted to go the fuck home to my husband and children. I said nothing. This wasn't his first time coming in here. I felt him when I slept at night. He would sneak in, stand over my bed, and watch me for about twenty minutes. I was a light sleeper because I was in a foreign place. The shit was creepy, but I didn't speak on it.

I became mute once they brought me to this room. Magnolia wasn't the only one with mental issues. I suffered from separation anxiety really bad, but I always kept it under control. Only Magnolia knew that about me. Hence, the reason I kept Zyrese and was with Magnolia so quickly back then was I was afraid of being alone, not lonely. I let Magnolia take control of almost everything, and he became my everything in a year's time because I didn't want to be alone. I broke down and told him years back that I would have been mute had he not saved me. I felt that if I was silent, no one would notice me, and time and time again, I failed miserably because it never happened.

"So, no answer for me?" he asked.

I looked at him and said nothing. His glare didn't waver, and neither did mine. We were in a staring match. He didn't know who he was fucking with, but he would find out the hard way or kill me first. If I didn't want to talk to nigga, then I wouldn't. He couldn't make me, that's for sure. He stood there rocking from side to side, dreads swaying with his body. His skin was a deep chocolate. Clear of any blemishes, the complete opposite of what I was used to. His eyes were hazel but had this look in them that could snatch a bitch's soul, but I still couldn't look away.

That wasn't it, though. There was something about his entire demeanor that was different. He wasn't overly masculine, but I knew it lived in him. He was humble but still a menace, if that made sense. I got that just from his actions. He and Magnolia were a lot alike, but he didn't know me. I remained quiet until he sat on the end of the bed and turned to look at me. I jumped at his sudden move.

"What's the problem? I won't hurt you. I don't have you here to hurt you, I promise."

Something about the way he said the shit made my legs shake but not in a turn me on way, more like a best friend way, and I didn't even know this nigga. He made me feel a little comfortable, but his wife didn't.

"You are hurting me by keeping me away from my family. I can't even talk to them to know if they're okay. That hurts here." I clutched my chest. "What if someone took your wife from you and held her captive against her will?" I asked him, and he looked at me, deep in thought.

"Then they would have her, but not for long," he answered, making his hand the shape of a cocking gun.

"This shit is bigger than you, princess. Your husband needs to be taught a lesson, a lesson that he will never forget," he added. "I have been watching him for a long time, and he doesn't love or appreciate you. I know about the things you both have done to each other. Would you call that love?" he asked.

I was surprised because how the fuck did he know about the shit we'd been through? And how could he watch from Haiti? I wanted to ask, but I was afraid of the answer.

"To answer the question that is lingering in your head, I have footmen in the United States on watch, but I also have drones in the sky that can see everything. I own fucking Haiti, and I can make anything happen. I know he hurt you when he fell in love with his therapist and all the shit that has been surrounding your marriage. It's like a black cloud has been lingering over your lives, and you can't catch a break."

This nigga was out of his mind, but I was intrigued. I sat there, listening to every word that fell from his mouth.

"I wouldn't hurt you because this entire situation had nothing to do with you, but I had to have you when I saw you on my drone. You were at your house, outside with your bathing suit on, and I knew I had to come up with something to get you next to me."

I thought about what he said and vividly remembered that day. I had the day off and decided to bask in some sun while everyone was gone from the house.

"You watched me?" I broke more silence.

"Yes, and it was a beautiful sight to see. I became obsessed with you. It was by sheer luck that Kadafi came to me about a deal with Magnolia, and I jumped on it. I knew he would bring you because you all never traveled alone. It was never one without the other. I did raise the price a little. Didn't think he would take the bait, but the nigga's ego wouldn't let him stop. When you all came to make the deal, I knew I had to do something to make you stay, but without him. Then, the plot thickened. There's more deeper shit going on, but I won't tell you today because it's not the time," he told me, and I hopped from the bed.

I didn't give a fuck what I had on because I needed to know the real reason I was here. I knew his lust wasn't the main reason. That shit was insane. I stood at the side of the bed, folding my arms under my breasts, and I watched him with evil eyes. He stood as well and watched my every move.

"That's bullshit, and you know it. I don't give a fuck about you watching because yo' wife is ugly as fuck, but she is fine, more like a trophy wife, so I get it." I thought the insult would make him tell me, but I was wrong.

He was in front of me in two point five seconds with his hand around my neck. He had me slightly lifted from the floor, and my feet were about to dangle.

"Don't talk about my fucking wife. I know she ain't the

baddest, and that's why I took the fucking baddest from a nigga who thought he had it all under control," he barked in my face, and I laughed on the inside.

He was strong, but not that fucking strong because his ass was struggling to hold me in his grip. He couldn't even choke me right. I wasn't even fucking breathless. This nigga was a fucking joke and weak. I rolled my eyes to the ceiling because I would be more out of breath from kicking and screaming than him hemming me up against the wall.

"You done? Because I would like my feet to touch the fucking floor soon before you choke me to death," I lied because he wasn't putting in no work.

Fuck, Magnolia made a bitch pass out before, so this was light work. He shook his head and chuckled, letting me down to the floor.

"I see why that nigga married you. You are a piece of work." He laughed, and I joined in. I couldn't help it because he was more breathless than me.

"If you knew the life I had before him, you would understand, but it's all good. You tried it," I told him and realized the nigga didn't have an accent like his wife.

I barely understood what the fuck she was saying while on the way to our destination, but I knew she was speaking of me because she would roll her eyes, but he talked like the typical hood nigga. That made my antennas go up, but I would keep quiet for now. His eyes gave me a twice-over, and my body shivered. I couldn't help it. The nigga was fine as fuck. He didn't ask about my life, and I wasn't about to volunteer shit because I wanted to know what he meant by the shit was bigger than me.

I pushed past him and went to the dresser to get a bigger shirt and a bra. The nigga had to like me a little because he got everything I fucking needed as far as clothes. He knew my bra size and everything. Shit was crazy, but I was grateful. I grabbed a shirt and bra, and when I turned around, he was standing there, watching me.

"Don't you have a wife to tend to and watch? Go look for her and bother her," I told him, and he didn't say shit.

He walked a little closer to me but not close enough to be in my personal space.

"She not here, and she's not who I wanna talk to right now. I got the best sight in the fucking house, so why would I leave? I already know how these look anyway because you leave little to the fucking imagination. I could almost imagine that you don't even have on panties under those tight-ass shorts you're wearing," he said, reaching out to pinch my nipple.

I didn't jump back fast enough, and he caught it. The shit felt good as hell. He knew it because he smiled, and my titties pebbled. I didn't say shit because I couldn't; he caught me red-handed. Something as small as a pinch of the breast had my clit tingling, and I didn't even know his ass. Either I missed my husband too much, or this nigga was gon' get the pussy with one false move. I didn't argue because he was right. It didn't matter if he stayed and watched or not because I wasn't ashamed of my body at all. I just didn't change in front of any man except my husband.

He backed up a little, giving me space, but he didn't stop staring at me. I didn't have a choice, so I took the shirt off and gave his ass a show. He wouldn't touch me because then I would fight his ass, and he would have to explain a black eye to his wife. I slid the shirt over my head, grabbed my bra, and hooked it around my back. I made sure to jiggle my breasts together before pulling the other shirt over my head. I wasn't changing my shorts, so he would have to deal with it. If this was where I would be for my time here, then I would walk around this bitch butt ass naked if I wanted to.

I pushed past him and went back to my bed, making sure to dig the left side of my shorts out of my ass for emphasis because I knew he was looking. I flopped back on the bed, and my mind went to my family. I knew they were worried. I also knew Magnolia was strategizing a master plan to get me out of this fucking mess. Then, my mind went to MJ. I hoped what he said to me wasn't true because my heart would break if it was.

"What's on yo' mind? You can talk to me." Khap snapped me out of my thoughts, and I rolled my eyes to the ceiling.

"You are not my fucking husband, and he is who I talk to. I don't even fucking know you." He walked over to the bed to sit the fuck on it again.

I didn't want his fucking company, but he insisted on giving it to me. The only device he let me have was a fucking Kindle. I knew he did it because all I could do with it was read books. I grabbed it off the nightstand and turned it on to tune him the fuck out, hoping he would leave.

"Yo' mouth will get you fucked up, but no, I am not yo' husband. If I was, you wouldn't be talking to me like that," he rebutted, and I started laughing.

"You are half my husband's size, and I fucked him up before." I paused "What's makes you think I can't beat yo' ass? Is it because you got guns? But we both know you wouldn't pull a fucking gun on little ole me," I told him, shaking my head. This nigga was delusional.

"Size don't matter, princess, and you are right. I wouldn't pull a gun on a woman, but I will do something else." He licked his lips, and I didn't like the way my body reacted to him. I shouldn't be attracted to his sexy ass, but I was.

"Can you please leave me alone like the fuck you been doing? I don't wanna fucking be here!" I yelled loud as fuck, and he laughed.

"But you will be here until I decide what I wanna do with you. You're a doctor, right?" he said, rubbing his chin.

I looked up at his face, and he was so fucking cute. His skin was perfect and looked soft. I shook thoughts from my head.

"You know that already because you did your homework. Now, can you please leave before yo' ugly ass wife comes in here and thinks the wrong thing? I would hate to have you witness me whipping her ass," I told him, giving attitude because I wanted him out of the same space as me.

"You can have it, princess, and I will get out of your space, but you can't run from me too much longer." He blew me an air kiss before getting up and walking out the door.

I didn't bother to lock it because he probably had a key to just about every room in this motherfucker. I turned my back, laying on my stomach, and searched for something to read on this small ass Kindle.

CHAPTER NINE

KHAP (KHAPRIANO)

I knew Princess would be hard to deal with, but I was up for the task. Her mouth made me want to kiss her and smack her ass at the same time. Her body is what caught a nigga off guard, and the fact that Magnolia brought his wife with him to handle business. To see her body in person had me ready to end my own marriage. Princess wasn't leaving Magnolia for shit, but I knew she held some type of attraction to me, even if she didn't want to admit it. The eyes never lie, and hers spoke volumes. She loved her husband, but she was lusting over me.

When Kadafi first told me about the deal Magnolia wanted with the guns, I thought about it long and hard. Either he didn't give a fuck or just didn't know, but his brother, Jahari, was fucking my sister. His wife burned their house the fuck down, but he left my sister inside. I told my sister not to go to the States without security, but she didn't listen. It was just she and I. My father was coming from the market a few years back with my mother in the car. I never knew them to have marital problems because, coming up, my father ran the gun empire. I don't know the conversation they were having in the car, but my father drove them off a cliff, ejecting my mother through the windshield and killing her instantly. He later died at the hospital from his injuries. They ruled it as a murder-suicide, and we moved on.

Zianda and I grew up together, and she was with me through everything in my life, even my transformation. I was born a woman, but I knew something had to be wrong because I had too much testosterone. As I grew up, I went through puberty and started to grow a beard like a man. My voice even got deep, like a man. The only thing I had for a woman was a pussy. Zianda knew that, but she was gay, so she stuck it out with me.

When my parents died, I had to take over. Everybody already thought I was a boy, so I went through with the sex change and turned myself fully into a man. I didn't have breasts, so I worked out religiously to turn the little I did have into muscle. The only people who knew that were my sister, Zianda, and the doctors who performed the procedure. The process was hard and painful, but it was worth it because I was standing in my truth. The problem was, I couldn't give my wife kids.

I loved Zianda because she never judged me when she knew the truth, but I wasn't in love with her. She only held shit down with a nigga because she felt like she paid her dues to support me when I needed her, so I was forever in debt to her. I understood her reasoning, but my feelings for her had long faded away. I can't remember the last time I was physically aroused by Zianda, but she didn't give a fuck. As long as she could spend my money and handle business alongside me without any threats, she was good. She had turned into a monster, and I couldn't control her, so I just let the shit happen. I had long ago accepted the fact that this marriage was more of convenience than love. We didn't even sleep in the same fucking room. She had her room, and I had mine, which was closer to Princess because I wanted to keep an eye on her. I was obsessed with her.

I was fucked up about what Jahari did to my sister, but it wasn't completely his fault. My sister shouldn't have been in that woman's home. She was pushing it, but that didn't surprise me because she was very impulsive. She had the little sister syndrome. She thought I would always come to her rescue, and I usually did, but that time, I was too late.

When Magnolia walked into my club for the exchange with his wife, I had every intention of it being a smooth transaction. I felt Zianda's entire body tense when Princess walked into the room. She commanded attention, and she didn't know it. I saw why Magnolia married her young ass. She had it all, beauty, brains, and body. I couldn't let her leave, so I had to come up with something to make her ass stay because I knew her husband would put up a fight. I didn't need his fucking money because I had generational wealth. At any time, I could stop my business and live off what I had, but I loved the thrill of supplying guns for the entire United States. I knew he had money, too, but then again, it was an ego thing with him because he knew my guns weren't going for that price per shipment. It was half of that.

I didn't want his money. Princess was who I wanted, and that's who I ended up getting. I knew I had started a war with this nigga, but he had other shit to worry about. His son was shot by some Chinese nigga who was trying to take over with his father, but I wouldn't let that happen. I was helping Magnolia, and he didn't even know it. After that shit that happened at his house, I sent my army to watch everything moving in the state. I knew the nigga could protect himself, but I was just the extra if he needed it. Even though I had his wife, I would still have his back because he and Kadafi were tight, so he was considered family as well.

I couldn't explain my fascination with Princess, but it was present and strong. She wasn't fucking with me, though. I could tell she was at peace here but would much rather be with her family. I was a selfish nigga, so I wouldn't let her go. I took everything that I thought she could use to communicate with her family because I knew they would come for her. Just like I had reach, so did her husband, and it was only a matter of time. I knew I couldn't get her to fall in love with me because her heart belonged to Magnolia, but I did want to taste the pussy; I just knew it was sweet. Her attitude was bad as fuck, but it made my dick hard. Not to even forget about her voluptuous ass body that I couldn't stop staring at.

If I thought I could put a fucking spell or perform a ritual on her ass, I would, but I knew she would fight against it. I would just let her cool off until she was ready to talk with some sense because she wasn't going anywhere. I walked down to my theatre room to watch my favorite movie. I had completed all my shipments today, and luckily, I didn't have to kill anyone because they had paid their dues. All my lieutenants had dropped off their bags of money, and I had my butler put them in the basement so I could count the shit later.

I sat down, put on *Shottas,* and rolled me a blunt. As soon as I sealed the blunt, I heard the door open. I knew it was wishful thinking, but I wished it was Princess. When I heard the clink of the heels, I knew it was Ziandra. She walked into the room, turning the lights on and pissing me off. She came into my view with tons of bags in her hand. I knew she wanted to show me what she bought with my fucking money. That was her thing.

Every time she went out with her dumb ass friends who used her, she would come home and show off everything she got to me like I cared. I would just look as she modeled everything, including the lingerie. She must have thought that shit would turn me on, but it didn't. She just didn't do it for me anymore, and I didn't think she had caught the shit yet. She dumped all the shit on the seats and stood in front of me with a smile a mile wide across her face. As long as she was happy, my house was happy.

She took off her clothes, tried the first dress on, and modeled it in front of me. I paused my movie, although I had seen it a million times.

"You like it, Khapriano?" She called my real name because I wasn't paying attention to her. My eyes were on her, but my mind was somewhere else. I really looked at her, and she frowned.

"What are you thinking about like that? I have been prancing in front of you for the past five minutes, and you never noticed. What the fuck is the problem?" she asked, and I knew where this conversation was going.

"Watch how you talk to me, girl. I was looking at you, but you do this shit every time you go shopping with yo' uppity ass friends. I get tired of seeing the same shit every time you go out and come back home with new shit. You never ask me to come with you like you used to. What, you out here fucking around or something? Is it some shit you don't want me to see?" I asked because it was true.

I had been going out shopping with her for a long time, but then it suddenly stopped. She had made new friends through my connect and started hanging out with their wives, but she left me out. At first, I was cool with it, but then the shit started happening too often, and I started to question it. She started to come home later and later, and it was starting to look very suspicious. I didn't voice it because I knew that one day my turn would come, and I didn't want her questioning my whereabouts.

"Oh, you getting out of line because that new bitch is here. You must be fucking her because she never comes out of that room, and don't think I don't look at the cameras," she said.

I knew she was lying because she didn't have access to the cameras in Zenobia's room. She never came out. Her food was always brought to her, and when she finished, the butler took the plate from her room. She thought I would bite the fucking bait, and I wouldn't. I was too smart for that, and she knew it.

"If I was fucking her, you would know, and I would tell you, so what the fuck are you lying for?" I got up and went into her personal space.

She had never talked to me like that. That was a giveaway that she was doing some shit behind my back. I was so close to her face that I inhaled her exhale.

"And if my memory serves me fucking correct, you wanted her to fucking stay, not me, but for what fucking reason? So, she could see how we living? Or do you wanna fuck her?" I had spoken some truth because her black ass face turned beet red.

She wanted her and was mad because she thought I was fucking her. She didn't say anything.

"You want to fuck her, don't you?" She tried to turn her head away from me, but she couldn't because I was too close. Her eyes went down.

"I knew you wanted to fuck her. That's why you wanted her here, but she ain't fucking gay, so all bets are off," I told her, and she backed away. She looked up at me as I towered over her.

"What the fuck you think you gon' do, then? Let's not

forget, under all that shit you got on, you are one of us." She tried to belittle me, but that shit wouldn't work. I knew what the fuck I was then, but I was sure now.

"I got a better fucking chance than you do, so find something safe to do before I end you," I said, picking up her bags and throwing them to the floor. "Pick that shit up and get the fuck out of my sight," I told her, and she shamefully bent down to pick all her shit up and dragged it out of my theatre.

I didn't care how I talked to her anymore because she had crossed the line. That was a first for her to throw in my face what the fuck I went through as far as my transition. She was big mad, but I couldn't let it bother me. Zianda had her own insecurities to deal with that didn't have shit to do with me. I unpaused my movie and continued to watch until it went off. I had faced two blunts and was still sitting there looking at a blank screen. The words Zianda said resonated in my ears and got the best of me.

I pulled my cellphone from my pocket and opened the app for the cameras that I had around my house. I first checked on my guards who were stationed around my estate because I didn't trust anyone, and it was late. Everybody was where they needed to be, so I moved to the cameras inside the house. I zoomed in on Zianda's room, and she was putting her things away with her phone glued to her ear. I wanted to listen in on her conversation but I chose not to.

Gone was the defeated and depressed look on her face. It was replaced with a smile so wide her cheeks could fall off, and she was blushing. She had found someone to occupy her time, and I was okay with that because I knew our marriage wouldn't last long anyway. I was over it and had been for some time, but her smiling like that on the phone meant another bitch or nigga had put that there.

I got up to close the door to the theatre for privacy and

then locked it. I sat back down and switched the camera to Princess's room. She was sitting on the bed, reading the little device I had bought her to keep her busy. I smiled as she lay crossways on her stomach, with her legs bent and crossed behind her. She looked so innocent, but I knew she wasn't, and that's what turned me on. She had to be the one to have the last say in everything, and she didn't cower under my words or stares. She took that shit to her chest.

Princess was a strong woman, and that's what I needed on my team. Ziandra used to be my strong woman, but along the way, she fell by the wayside and became this weak bitch that I didn't recognize. I watched her for a minute until I noticed her lift herself off the bed. She hadn't eaten yet and refused the food that my butler had offered earlier because she wasn't hungry, per my butler telling me earlier. She went to the dresser and pulled out those shorts that had her ass spilling from the bottom and a short T-shirt. She went to the bathroom, and I cursed myself because I didn't have cameras installed there. I didn't need them, or so I thought. She laid her clothes out on the bed and went back into the bathroom to start her shower. I turned the volume on because I saw her lips moving and wanted to know what she was saying or singing.

I watched as she took every piece of clothing off, and my dick got hard. When she pulled her shorts off, I changed the angle of the camera so I could get a full view of her pussy, and it looked fat and juicy. My mouth watered because I knew that peach was sweet. My hand went into my pants as she disappeared into the bathroom. I could hear the shower running, but I still heard her unique voice singing.

"Damn near lost it all. Back against the wall gave so much of me, losing myself through it all. Trying to fill you up, pouring from an empty cup, lost so much of myself in your game called love."

I had heard that song before but couldn't remember where.

The way Princess sang it with so much pain and hurt, I knew she meant every word that came out of her mouth. I continued to listen to her sing as I stroked my meat until it was as hard as a brick.

After a few minutes, I heard the shower turn off, then she walked out of the bathroom, soaked with her locs in a bun, butt ass naked. I stroked myself harder with thoughts of her pussy wrapped around my dick and her singing in my ear. She was fucking beautiful. From her head to her toes, she was perfect as fuck. She let herself air dry, then started with her lotion and rubbed it on every part of her body.

"Fuck."

I came in my hand, and I grabbed the bucket to clean myself up. I could look at her and come, but I wanted to feel her. I often came in here to watch porn because I didn't want to fuck Zianda, so I was prepared. I never stopped watching her, though. She slid the shorts and shirt on and looked around the room as if she knew someone was watching her. She would never find the camera because nobody knew where they were, not even Zianda.

I was surprised when she slipped on her slippers, walked to the door, and opened it to go out. I watched every camera that she walked by until she got to the first floor, and she was searching. My guess was her ass got hungry and decided to roam the house for the kitchen to find something to eat. I watched as she found her way to the kitchen, but she didn't turn on the light. She was probably scared, and I knew this was my chance.

I fixed myself and got up to leave the theatre. I took the shortcut to get to the kitchen where she was. Standing by the wall, I watched her for a minute. She had the fridge wide open, but I couldn't see anything but the top of her locs because she was so short. The light from the fridge lit up the entire right side, so I knew she was searching for something to eat. She was shuffling stuff around like a little mouse, searching for food. I stood silently before making my way toward her, taking slow steps so I wouldn't scare her or make her run. I knew she was a runner because her calves were thick as fuck, and I thought about them being wrapped around my neck. I crept toward the closed side of the door and snuck up behind her. She squeaked.

"Oh, my God, Khap. What are you?"

Before she could get another word out, I shushed her with my finger. I didn't want her talking too loudly and causing someone to come snooping. I had something to do first. My other hand went around her waist, turning her to me.

"If I move my finger, don't say shit."

Her eyes got big as saucers, but she quickly shook her head up and down. I removed my finger and replaced it with my lips. She tried to push me at first, but when she invited my tongue into her mouth, I knew I had her. I swirled my tongue in and out of her mouth while holding the back of her head. She was stiff at first but then fell into the groove and started to kiss me back. I swear a bolt of electricity went through my spine as she grabbed my dreads, pulling me further into her. Both of my hands grabbed her healthy hips in a kissing frenzy. I knew she had to stay here with me, or I wouldn't survive it. I sucked on her tongue as we fought for control of the other but couldn't because we were both losing.

"Fuck," she moaned in my mouth as I sucked her lips.

Her shit was so soft and juicy that I could only imagine what her southern lips were like.

"You gotta stop this shit," she told me through kisses, but her body was saying otherwise. Her body wanted this, but her heart was with her husband, and I understood that. I never wanted her to second guess what she was doing, but this was my time, even if it wasn't for a long time, and I was going to take it.

"Your mouth is saying we gotta stop, but yo' lips still connecting to mine, and I know that pussy wet as fuck for me," I told her, and she moaned.

"Shhhh, be a good girl, and I got something for you," I told her, and she looked at me.

I was hypnotized. She had a hold on me, and I hadn't even gotten to know her. Looking sexy as hell, she sucked in her bottom lip. She just didn't know it, but I was about to swallow the whole bottom half of her body. I knew I didn't have much time, but I wanted to take my time and live in this moment with her because I knew I wouldn't get this chance again.

I got down on my knees, pulling her shorts with me. I started with her feet, using my mouth to glide my tongue up her ankle toward her inner thigh while my hand massaged the other. Her legs trembled, but I would hold her up if she let me. Her head fell back against the fridge, and I chuckled on the inside. I tongue sucked her clit, and she gasped loudly and held her breath.

"Quiet, Princess," I told her and put my face in her dripping tunnel. Her shit was splashing waterfalls.

I lifted her leg over my shoulder for better access, and my tongue dug deeper into her. Her clit sat on my nose as my tongue played with her insides. She rolled her hips against my face as I stilled my tongue and let her ride the wave. She was shaking and grinding like a stripper at the same time. She reached down to hold my face exactly where she wanted it, and her clit started to jump in my mouth. I knew she was about to rain on me. Two thumps, and her clit was washing my face clean. I caught as much as I could with my mouth, but the rest leaked down my chin. Her body continued to shake as she held my head in place until she finished.

She stood there in shock as she looked down at me, embarrassed. Then, she quickly grabbed her shorts and ran off to her room, if she remembered where the fuck it was. I wiped my mouth with the back of my hand, smiling because I knew I could break her down with my head alone, and I was just getting started.

CHAPTER TEN
DAISY

I had been in this shed for I don't know how long and didn't know what the fuck was going on. Nobody had given me any information on what the fuck was going on with MJ, and I was mad as hell. I had nothing to do with what the fuck Trahan and his friends did, but I couldn't get Zenobia to see that. I knew they hated Lotus, but that was her, not me. We were the complete opposite, and I hated that I was being judged because of her. I loved MJ with everything in me and wanted to know what the fuck was going on.

If I had my way, my parents would have been dead a long time ago, but I learned that you couldn't kill bad grass. Their names would follow me everywhere I went, and I hated it. Living in this shed wasn't that bad, but I knew I couldn't get away because it was like Fort Knox around this bitch. I just wished that someone could tell me something about what was going on.

The good thing about this shit was that they weren't treating me like shit. I still had food to eat, but I didn't have a phone. I had clothes to wear, and the shed was made like a mini apartment. Everything was in one room, and I was okay with that. I didn't even know what time or day it was because no one came to tell me shit. I thought about ways to get out of this bitch, but if I did, I would get shot down like a dog for trying to escape. I did, however, have a radio that they let me listen to, and that gave me a little peace.

I sat in the middle of the queen-sized bed, eating my mac and cheese with fried chicken that was brought to me as I listened to the music that played. It was MJ and my favorite song. I closed my eyes and pictured us dancing in the middle of the floor without a care in the world.

Somebody real is heard to find.
Somebody worth all yo time.
Someone who tells you the truth.
Someone who loves you for you
Someone who loves all of your flaws and.
Doesn't impose, try to control them.
Let you be free, doesn't deceive and.
They give you a chance to believe in something.
Is that too much?
Cause I been on a search and I'm losing my hope.

Tink's "Treat Me Like Somebody" blared through the small speaker as my eyes remained closed and my imagination ran wild. I pictured myself in a white wedding dress and MJ in a white tuxedo. It was just us dancing to that song because it described our relationship.

When I first encountered MJ, I had just cut shit off with Trahan. I was tired of his cheating ways and thinking it was okay to put his hands on me and disrespect me. I cut him off, and he couldn't handle it. It wasn't a messy breakup. I simply didn't want him anymore. I was tired of him, and I knew there was better out there for me. MJ and I started out as friends, with me venting to him about the antics that Trahan would use to hurt me physically. MJ was there every step of the way during my heartbreak. He even told bits and pieces about his life... well, the parts he knew about his family. I could tell he didn't know much, and that was a good thing because I didn't want to know.

I knew who his parents were, and I had dreaded the day that I had to meet them. I tried to keep our relationship under wraps for as long as I could, but the cat was out of the bag, and this shit happened because of my dead sister. One of them killed her, but I didn't care because I wasn't there to avenge her murder. I was simply in love with their son.

I heard the door creak open, and I got scared because I didn't know who it was. A big, burly man walked in with a woman beside him, and I assumed that was his wife. He was sexy, but I didn't think too much of it because his wife looked crazy. I believe they were at the party, but my mind couldn't register. Fuck I can't even remember if I was at the party. I just looked at them without saying a word. They stood there with all black on. The man had on a hoody, jeans, and boots. His hoodie covered half his face. The woman was wearing a black Lululemon tracksuit. I knew because I had the same one.

"Take that shit off before you scare the damn girl. She might think we are coming in here to fucking kill her, Bear," she told him and pulled the top part of his hood off, displaying his face.

"Janiya, I do what the fuck I want to do. I don't know if we can trust her or not," they argued back and forth.

"If she is still alive, then he must trust her, but we ain't here for the bullshit," she said and looked at me.

"Get up and gather yourself. We got somewhere to be."

I wondered if everything was okay with MJ because I

hadn't heard anything about him. I quickly gathered everything I wanted and rushed to the door. I stopped when I was halfway out.

"Where is MJ? Why didn't he come to get me?' I asked them, and they both looked at me.

Janiya grabbed my arm, pulling me close to her side.

"He is no longer living. We are about to fly out to New Orleans for his funeral."

I couldn't believe what the fuck I was hearing. There was no way he was dead. The doctor said he would recover. I had just found the love of my life, and he was abruptly taken from me. I screamed and lost my balance because I couldn't control my emotions.

"Pick her up, Bear, and bring her to the plane," I heard her tell him, and I felt my body being lifted in the air.

I couldn't believe I had lost the one person who I knew for sure loved me the most. I had so many questions, but I already knew the answers. Trahan and his family gon' have to die, even if I had to do the shit myself.

CHAPTER ELEVEN
ZYRESE

"Don't do that, Reesy," Jadior said as I tried to kiss her neck.

Since the day we made groceries, we had been inseparable. If we didn't have class, we spent time together. She did her work while I painted, and we were making it work. I still had my eye on Trahan because that nigga was dipping in and out of my space, but he had never caught wind of Jadior being with me. It was like every time he came to the crib, she wasn't there, and I was thankful for that because I didn't know what we were doing. We enjoyed spending time with each other but that was as far as it went. We hadn't even kissed fully yet, but she was there almost every day.

Currently, I was painting her on the empty spot on my wall. It was a picture of the way she was sitting with books scattered all over my bed. I kept fucking up because my mind was focused on somewhere else. My mind was on my family. I wondered if MJ was okay and where the fuck my sister was. Those were questions that I needed answers to but refused to ask because I was afraid of the answer.

"Fuck, man!" I threw my brush down to grab another with white paint.

I painted over the entire spot to start over again. I knew it would take a while for it to dry, so I decided to pick her brain about some shit. I plopped next to her on the bed. Her glasses were so cute on her face, and they made her look like a real schoolgirl. The shit was sexy and made me feel things I hadn't felt before. I knew I had a dick, but the way it reacted to her was a first. My shit got hard every time I thought about or even saw her, but I knew how to control it. I lay back on the bed, and she was so engrossed in her schoolwork that she didn't notice me watching her. She was a work of art, literally. I could paint every version of her if she let me.

Jadior looked up and noticed that the wall was clear, and her eyes came back toward mine. She removed the glasses from her face and looked at me.

"What happened? I thought you were painting. What's wrong?' she asked, genuinely concerned.

I wanted to trust her, but I wasn't so sure because shit was moving too fast. She sensed my hesitation and closed her book to turn to me. Climbing up on my body, she straddled me, and I felt my dick getting hard. I tried to control it, but whatever perfume she had on her body invaded my nostrils. She sat straight on my hard dick, and I knew she felt it because she started to smile down at me.

"You good?" she asked.

I nodded my head up and down because I could answer her with words. I grabbed her hips, trying to remove her from my body because the pressure from her heated middle was too much for me, and I was scared of what might happen. She grabbed my wrist, trying to stop me.

"What if I like this feeling, Zyrese?" She let go of my wrist and ran her hands up my chest. All this shit was new to me, and I didn't think she knew that. I was a fucking nervous wreck, but I didn't think she caught it. She leaned her body down, titties touching my bare chest, with her lips inches from mine.

"Don't be scared. Just do what comes naturally. I know you a virgin, Zyrese. It shows, and I'm okay with that. I wanna be your first and only," she said and pecked my lips.

"You done this before?" I had to ask but it didn't matter one way or the other. She was fucking with me now. Her eyes never wavered when she answered me.

"Only once before, and he broke my virginity, but that was a year ago," she answered, and I believed her.

"I want this with you, though." Her soft voice stirred something in my heart.

"I never even kissed before," I confessed. I felt foolish, but I didn't think girls would be into niggas with autism, so I kept to myself while I was in school.

"I'm about to teach you," she said, sucking my lips into hers. Her tongue slid into my mouth, and I thought I was in heaven.

I followed suit and swirled my tongue into her mouth as my hands gripped the sides of her waist. She turned her head to the side and kissed me deeper, making my dick harder and harder. She began this little grinding shit against my dick, and it felt so fucking good that I thought I would explode. I stopped her movement because I didn't want to make a mess in my pants.

"What's wrong?" she asked with concern etched on her beautiful face.

"My dick is hard as fuck, and it feels like it's about to bust. I can't control it." I was honest with her because I didn't know shit about what the fuck my body was doing. She stared into my eyes.

"Don't worry about him. I'll take care of him." She didn't move from my body.

Jadior pulled her shirt over her head and threw it to the floor. She pushed all her books to the floor and used her hands to unhook her bra, setting her titties free. They sat up perfectly without a bra. I thought I was dreaming because I had thought about this since the first time I saw her. Her nipples were hard as rocks.

"Touch them. Everything on my body now belongs to you." She moaned and grabbed my hands, putting them on her breasts. They were soft and plump as I rubbed them and pinched her nipples.

Her head fell back, and I kept that sight of her in my mind to paint later. She was enjoying the way my hands felt, and I didn't know what the fuck I was doing. She rocked her body back and forth, biting her top lip like my dick was inside of her.

"Damn, that feels so good." She moaned, and I was about to lose it.

Her hair was wild and all over her face, giving her a vixen look. I had never witnessed her in this element, but it was a sight for sore eyes. She lifted up a little, and I felt her hands on my meat. I froze.

"Too much?" she asked, her eyes glued to me.

I didn't know how to answer her. It wasn't too much, but the sensation that her hand was giving my dick was definitely too much.

"Do you want me to stop?" she asked because I didn't answer the first question. I couldn't answer the second one either.

"Nah, keep going." I didn't recognize my own voice because it was deeper than usual. She lifted up a little, pulled her panties off, and threw them aside.

I didn't know she had any on or how she'd gotten them off

because she was straddling me. I didn't question it. I felt her warm southern lips wrap around my dick, and I knew she would be the death of me.

"I promise I will take you slow, Reesy," she called me by my nickname, and I couldn't take it anymore.

She slid down my pole, inch by inch, and I felt like I was suffocating. Her walls were so tight and warm. I was sure to nut prematurely.

"Wait, we need a condom," I told her, and her eyes popped open.

"No, we don't because you are going to be my husband. And you won't get me pregnant because I am on birth control," she told me.

I nodded my head up and down as she went down further and further.

"You so fucking big. I don't think he can fit." She stopped halfway down. I didn't know where the fucking confidence came from, but I had it.

"Be a good girl and take your dick because it belongs to you now." I gripped her hips tightly as she went further until she reached the base.

"Shit, Jadior," I moaned like a bitch, but I didn't care because I was her bitch.

I could be my authentic self with her, and I knew I was falling in love. This moment just sealed the deal. Her juices wet me up, and I didn't care because I wanted all of her. She could rain down on me if she wanted to, and I would happily receive it. She started rocking back and forth with a slight bounce, and I was stuck.

"Fuck me back," she said, and I didn't know what to do.

I did what came naturally and sat up, grabbing her waist. She was thick but not fat, so I knew I could lift her. I lifted her up and down on my dick at a slow pace.

"Dammmnn, boy. Ummmm," she moaned, driving me crazy. She was so vulnerable, and I was slowly losing everything inside me.

"Your pussy gon' make a nigga crazy. This shit is like heaven. I can't get enough," I told her in return because it was true.

I could live in this feeling forever, but I knew this wasn't my reality. I didn't know what would happen after this moment was over, nor did I care because I was enjoying it. I felt all the blood rushing to the tip of my dick and knew I was about to nut. My shit started thumping inside her, and she started to move faster.

"You gon' make me nut, Zyrese?" The way my name lazily rolled off her tongue was just what I needed for the nut to spit inside her.

Her walls contracted around my shit, so she must've been about to nut as well. We moaned loud as fuck, and we both let loose at the same time. She fell against my chest, both our bodies full of sweat, chests heaving up and down. After our breathing went back to normal, she lifted her head and looked at me. We both started laughing at an unspoken joke. We didn't speak on what we had just done, but she did make something clear.

"You're mine now. I don't give a fuck if you paint on my skin. That shit don't matter to me, Zyrese. I want you with me." She was so possessive, and it was turning me on.

"What had you so angry that you painted over the picture of me? Did you mess it up or something? What's on your mind?" she asked, moving my dreads to the back but keeping one in her hand to play with.

I mulled over in my head about whether I wanted to let her inside that part of my life. That's the part nobody knew about. I didn't share the shit that went on in our family with anyone, but this would be a test of her loyalty. I would tell her bits and pieces of it. I closed my eyes and started explaining what happened when I went home for the holidays.

"Oh, my God, Zyrese. Is he okay? Isn't Trahan your friend? Why would he do such a thing?" she spit question after question, and I knew I should have kept it to myself.

Jadior didn't live the life I lived. She hadn't seen the shit I'd seen. We were from different sides of the track, and I didn't want to taint her with the lifestyle that was given to me.

"I don't know because I left. I felt suffocated and needed to come back to my comfort zone, and that's here at school. I don't know what's going on with my sister or even where she is, but I feel like something bad has happened, and no one wants to tell me about it because I might crash out. I love my sister with everything in me, and I haven't laid eyes on her since her trip with her husband. I know he wouldn't hurt her because he loves her too much, but I think something happened, and they are hiding it from me, so I had to come back to school for peace of mind until he calls me." I left out the part about Trahan because she didn't need to know all that.

I told her more than I should have already, and that wasn't good because I didn't know her intentions with me. Yeah, she said I was hers, but she had to earn my trust, just like I had to earn hers. After that conversation, we just lay in silence in our own thoughts. I didn't know what she was thinking, but my thoughts were on my sister and killing this nigga Trahan for fucking with my family.

Bam bam bam.

I heard the banging on my door. I wasn't expecting anyone, so I didn't know what the fuck was going on. Jadior grabbed the covers and covered herself while I pulled my joggers on and grabbed my gun from under my pillow. Her eyes got big with surprise, but she didn't ask any questions. Before I could get to the door, it opened, and in walked Jahari and Teedy Amerika.

"Boy, if you don't put that damn gun up, Imma whip yo' ass. Why do you have one anyway? Let me guess, Magnolia." She shook her head and pushed me out of the way, with Jahari following close behind her.

I didn't want them to see Jadior, but I didn't have a choice because they barged in my shit, and I knew not to be disrespectful because she would punch me in my shit. They walked in, looking around at the paintings on my wall and everywhere else.

"I see you still like to paint on other people's shit, huh? Magnolia gon beat yo ass boy. You just don't learn lessons at all, but the shit looks nice." Jahari laughed, shaking his head.

I tried to get in front of them to block them from going into my room, but it was too late. I wish they had sent Mhyesha and Gianni, but that was wishful thinking. Teedy Amerika went toward my room, and I tried to hurry and block her.

"Zyrese, if you don't move the fuck out my way. What are you in here hiding?" She pushed me out of the way and walked into my room.

"Bae, come see. Zyrese got a girl in his bed. This your girlfriend Rese? She looks a little familiar, but she's pretty."

I didn't know what to say, so she turned to Jadior.

"Umm, Miss Ma'am, you fucking my nephew?" she asked Jadior, and her face turned pink.

"If that's what you call it, but we made love," she answered in her soft voice.

"Finally! Fuck, I thought yo' old ass wasn't gon' never get no pussy, nigga." Jahari walked up to me and dapped me up.

I wanted to laugh at the look on Jadior's face because it was utter embarrassment.

"What was the reason for the surprise visit? Y'all heard

from my sister? And how is MJ?" I asked them, and they looked at each other like they were deaf mutes. I knew shit must have been bad for them to come all the way to the school instead of calling me.

"It's about MJ, nephew. He didn't make it," Amerika said low, but I heard her.

I knew she wasn't saying what I thought she was saying.

"The fuck you mean he didn't make it? Where was he going?" I asked her, confused.

"He died a few days ago. He was dead when you left to come back to school." She continued to shoot daggers in my heart.

MJ was my best fucking friend. I was so angry I couldn't even cry about it. My mind went to my sister and Magnolia. I knew they were losing their minds.

"Where is my sister? Why didn't she come up here to tell me?" I kept asking questions. Fuck it, I wanted to know everything.

"Nah, Zyrese, Magnolia gon' have to explain that one because it ain't for us to tell," Jahari said.

That made my blood fucking boil. They had known me long enough to know that I hated secrets, especially when shit was about my sister.

"Get dressed, pack some shit, and meet us at the car. Don't worry too much about clothes because we got that handled. If you bringing your new girlfriend with you, she gon' need to give Amerika her size, so we can get her right as well," Jahari said, and they walked out the door.

I wanted to stop them and ask them what the fuck was going on, but I didn't because I didn't want to know. I would just follow instructions. I went back to the room where Jadior was right where I left her in the bed.

"Look, I know you got class and shit, and I don't know

what the fuck is going on with my family, but I gotta go. I can leave the key, and you can stay." I was about to finish my sentence, but she stopped me.

"Whatever it is, I'm riding with you. It looks serious, and you might need me for whatever. So, tell me what I need to do in order to be by your side, Zyrese," she said in the most sincere tone. My heart skipped a beat.

"Well, Jahari told me that if you were coming, to give my Teedy your size, and she will handle the rest. Right now, we gotta grab what we can and leave with them because I got a feeling that we gon be out the state for a while and out the way," I told her.

She sprang from the bed. We got dressed, grabbed what we could, including our phones, and headed out the door to the truck. My stomach churned as I looked at Amerika with her dark-covered shades. She was hiding something from me, and I knew she wouldn't tell me.

"Where we going, Teedy?" I had to know because we were going in the opposite direction of the house.

"To the strip. We about to fly out to New Orleans. Now, stop asking questions. You got yo' gun with you?" Jahari asked me. I raised my shirt, and he nodded his head in approval.

Amerika looked at Jadior. "You look familiar, but I can't place your face. I hope you know what type of family you signed up for because we don't play or do bullshit," she told her.

Jadior nodded her head and looked at me. I didn't have shit to say; I knew first-hand how my teedy and my sister got down. I just hope Jadior was ready.

CHAPTER TWELVE
MAGNOLIA

Three days. Three fucking days that my son had been dead, and I hadn't moved his body out of the room he was in. I couldn't believe it. There was no way the world would be that fucking cruel that it would take my son from me. I shielded him from everything that I thought could bring him harm, and it still knocked on his front door. It was crazy to me and behind a fucking female. I wanted to kill that bitch Daisy, but it wasn't her fault, and I had yet to hear her side of the story. But I already knew what the fuck Trahan wanted. He and his father wanted territory that they weren't gon' get. If I had to go out like Cleo on *Set It Off*, I would die before I let those Chinese motherfuckers come from China and take over.

As I lay in bed with my dead son, my body was slowly leaving me. I had taken so many pills that I had become numb. I needed my wife, and it was sad that I couldn't function without her. I needed her presence, and I couldn't get that. I had yet to tell Mhyesha what the fuck happened, although she probably already knew. She was standing by the window and had been that way since she got here, trying to get answers from me that I didn't want to give.

I knew she wanted to help, but I wouldn't let her because she had retired and settled down with Gianni. I was a grown fucking man, and my house was not in order, but I would get it there by any means. First, I had to shake this demon off my back. I lay my big ass in that bed with my son. I looked up at his face, and his lips were a light shade of blue, so I knew it was real. He was gone. His body was stiff, with his eyes tightly closed. I couldn't accept it. The world had woken up a beast.

"Come on, Mahsyn, we gotta call the coroner and make the funeral arrangements. And how the fuck is my daughter-in-law kidnapped? Where the fuck is your antennas nigga? How the fuck did that even happen?" she asked for the hundredth time, and I didn't answer her.

I was defeated because I didn't protect her. I didn't know what the fuck was going on or what the fuck they were doing to her over there, and it was killing me. Brick after brick just kept dropping on my body, and it was becoming too heavy for me to hold.

"Ma, I can't talk about it because I couldn't protect her, and you wouldn't understand," I told her, and I felt her walking over to the bed.

She stood over me in the bed with MJ and stared.

"He is turning blue, Mahsyn. He can't stay here forever, and you gotta stop taking those fucking pills so you can function. You gotta be strong right now, and you looking very fucking weak. You got an entire army waiting on you to say the word, and they will go get Zenobia wherever she may be," she told me, but I wasn't trying to hear that shit because I had to strategize a fucking plan to get my wife home safe and untouched.

I had so much going on, so doing all this shit in one day was impossible. My heart was hurting, slowly breaking with each minute, hour, and day that passed. My world was falling apart, and I didn't know what the fuck to do about it. I couldn't control it. I was out of my body, and the only thing keeping me sane was the fucking pills I kept popping to numb my pain. I felt a yank on my shoulder.

"Look, Mahsyn, I know you hurting, but we can fix this shit. You are not alone, but what the fuck you not gon' do is let my grandson sit here and fucking rot for your own selfish reasons. He deserves for his soul to be at peace, and you need to get yourself together. You laying here with him like this is prolonging the inevitable, and we know what has to happen. There will be a lot of bloodshed in the streets behind this one, and I need you on yo' shit because you looking really fucking weak right now, and that's not who I raised," she said to my back because I refused to turn around to face her.

She was telling the truth, but I didn't want to hear it. Had I not even started the gun shit, my wife would be here, and I could have handled Trahan and Ming Ming myself because I knew they were lurking. I just couldn't see them. I wanted their heads on a platter, and I would be the one to do it because this shit was personal. If the pussy was that good and you wanted the territory that fucking bad, then have that shit because it wasn't worth my fucking family.

"I can't leave him. He needs me. I gottta wait for him to wake up."

I knew I was delusional, but I still believed that my son wasn't fucking dead. I knew somewhere inside his body, he had life, and I could feel it. He had to because the hurt I felt would turn me into The Incredible Hulk.

"His soul is in heaven, Mahsyn. He wouldn't want you acting like this. We gotta get him to his final resting place, and you gotta be strong enough to do it. We gon' get his body airlifted to New Orleans so you can get yourself together. I already called my people at Davis Funeral Home in New Orleans, and they are ready to accept his body," she told me, and reality really started to set in. I couldn't believe it.

"He took Zenobia, Ma, and I don't know how to get her back," I whispered, but I knew she heard me.

"Who the fuck took her, and where were your antennas when the fuck they took her?" she asked me, and I relayed the entire story to her.

"You mean to tell me that my Nobby in Haiti with those crazy ass Haitians behind some fucking guns that you were willing to pay for?" she asked.

"No, it's bigger than that. When Amerika burned their house down because Jahari was fucking some female, that female was the nigga Khap's sister," I told her. "And when we went for the exchange, he didn't want my money. He wanted my wife. Then the doctor—"

"That you fucking killed," she cut me off.

"Called my phone, telling me that MJ wasn't breathing, and I later found out that one of his nurses was one of Khaps people, so all this shit was a setup to get back at my family. I don't know what the fuck to do, Ma. I'm out of fucking options, and too much shit is happening for me to make any kind of move. Trahan is running wild. I got Zyrese on him, but I need my wife." Tears came out of my eyes every time I thought about Zenobia and what the fuck they could be doing to her.

"Stop that fucking crying and get yo' ass up and handle business. You let me worry about getting Zenobia back. You need to get yo' ass up, clean up, and get yo' shit together because my grandson is going home in the city he grew up in. I already got my people lined up to take him home, but you gotta get it together. Don't ever let nobody see you fucking weak. You stand tall like the man you are because this shit will be over soon. I can't bring MJ back, but your wife will be fucking back," she scolded me like I was a child. Then, she reached over to help me from the bed. Her small frame packed a lot of power.

"And yo' ass stank. Go take a shower. I had everybody get their suits for his funeral. They just waiting on you," she told me, and that made me feel a little better.

I was still a little pissed at Jahari because of this shit, but I couldn't be too mad because he didn't know that Amerika was gon' burn their fucking house down. The nigga was fighting for his life as well.

I dragged myself to the shower and took my time cleaning myself. I knew I wouldn't have time for a barber, so I opted to line myself up to look presentable. After getting out of the shower, I noticed my suit bag with Gucci on it, so I knew somebody got me right. I threw on my joggers, a tee, socks, and slippers for the flight back to New Orleans, a place that I left a long time ago.

If my mother planned this, then I knew the fucking hood was about to show out because we owned New Orleans. I just hated that I had to go back under these circumstances. I packed everything I would need and grabbed my twin 9s, tucked them in the holsters, and walked out of my room.

I watched as some men carried a black body bag down the stairs and out the door. My wife didn't even know our son was dead, and it pained me to know she wouldn't make it to the funeral. Then, there was Daisy. She didn't deserve the treatment that we were giving her. I knew she was Lotus' sister, but she wasn't her and wasn't a threat to me. She deserved to be there for everything.

I looked over the stairway banister, and all my soldiers were standing at attention. Some I didn't recognize, while others I hadn't seen in years. Mhyesha even bought some of her own. In the midst of them were Khaza, Endymion, and

Kadafi with their wives dressed in all black. My heart became full because I thought they'd left and didn't come back.

"Nigga, we family, so we move as a unit. The other couples went to notify Daisy and Zyrese and get them to the plane. I heard about the shit with Lotus, but I didn't think Daisy was anything like her. She loved MJ and deserved to be there, too. We were just waiting on you," Endymion said, and everybody else nodded.

This was too fucking much, and I didn't know how to handle it. All roads led back to my wife because she wasn't here, but I guess some things I had to do without her. I just prayed that she was still alive after all this shit was over. I needed her to be, or I would die from a broken heart. She was my everything, and I couldn't lose her. She told me a storm was brewing, but I never thought I would be going through it without her. I walked down the stairs, and everybody was silent. Mhyesha and Gianni were on each side of me. They spread like the Red Sea as I walked past them with my head down.

"Nah, chin up because we gon' get her," Endymion said as I walked out the door.

I didn't have to worry about locking it because I left my stronger soldiers behind, just in case some shit popped off.

The ride to the strip was a solemn and quiet one because I was high as fuck, and I didn't have anything to say. Gianni and Mheysha were closest to me, and everybody else was in their own world. My mind was foggy, but I could function for this.

"His funeral will be tomorrow. Everything is already set up, so all you have to do is show up. I know this shit is bittersweet, son, but trust yo' momma. I got you. The suit that you are wearing is the same one MJ will have on. I had Cynthia take the kids out and buy them royal blue dresses and everything they needed for this. If you want a repast, it's there. If not, I will tell everyone to get the fuck," she told me straight up, and I shook my head up and down.

"Nah, we gon' celebrate him because he was an innocent soul. I shielded him as much as I could from this life, and he still got caught up in it over some shit that a nigga couldn't let go of, but it's bigger than that. His paw wants what's mine, and he will never get it," I told Mhyesha as the flight took off and we headed back to where I was raised.

Once we got off the plane, we all gathered and got into individual cars, but we agreed to meet at Mhyesha's house. Her shit had been renovated over the years because she refused to leave the city, so it had enough rooms for all of us as couples. The block was already jumping when we pulled up like the army. The block stopped when we pulled up, but I didn't give that shit too much of my attention because I knew they knew what the fuck was going on. They probably knew before we even touched down because New Orleans was so small that everybody knew everybody's business in the city.

We all got out with our suit bags and shoes and went into the house. The ladies walked in front of us, but I stopped Zyrese before he could go any further.

"That's the girl you drew on your iPad?" I asked him, and he nodded.

"Watch her. I'll tell you her story at a later date because now is not the time or the place. If you fucking with her, then fuck with her, but get to know her a little more first." I tried to walk off, but he stopped me.

I knew what he was about to ask me, and I knew I had to give him a straight answer, but I had to make him understand in his own way.

"What happened to my sister, Magnolia? Why is she not here? Where is she? And I don't want no watered-down version," he told me.

I pulled him aside to explain to him. He told his lil friend to go ahead and gave her his suit bag and shoes. She looked at him and walked ahead with everybody. I could be tripping, but it was something about her that I didn't trust.

"What's your friend's name?" I tried to change the subject, but I knew he paid attention too much to forget.

He watched as she walked into the house.

"Jadior, and I think I'm falling in love with her. I had sex with her for the first time." He was so oblivious to the shit that was done when he was younger, but he was about to find out. I didn't want to do it now, but he needed to know before moving forward with anything pertaining to her.

"Listen, I need to tell you something about yo' friend because I see the same look in your eye that I saw in Zenobia's when she looked at me, so I know you falling in love," I told him, and he smiled.

"A few years ago, I had a therapist named Dior because of some shit that me and yo' sister was trying to work through, but I needed the extra help. Long story short, I fell in love with Dior, and Nobby killed her. Yo friend Jadior is her younger sister, so like I said, watch her. She didn't just fall from the fucking sky and into yo' lap. I know you had been watching her from afar, but I'm sure she had been watching you as well, so be careful, and don't say too much, or you know what you gotta do," I told him, and he agreed.

"My sister killed a bitch over you before?" he asked.

"Yeah, and you'd be surprised by how many niggas I had to put down because they thought they were going to fuck with my wife, not knowing her husband was crazy as fuck and would shed a lot of blood behind her. Ain't a fucking thing off limits when it comes to matters of the heart. Remember that." I dapped him up, but he stopped me.

I thought I had that nigga's mind off Zenobia because I

didn't want to explain that shit. He didn't forget shit, but I didn't expect him to.

"You sure you wanna know?" I asked him just in case he changed his mind.

"What, she left you or some shit?"

I could have said yeah, but I couldn't lie to him. He didn't deserve that shit.

"Look, we went to a meeting with this nigga in Haiti to do an exchange for some weapons. I went to pay him, but he didn't want money. He wanted Zenobia instead. We were outnumbered, and I got eyes on her, so she good. No harm is being done to her." I lied because I didn't want him to worry.

"So, why y'all can't just go get her? MJ was her son, too," he asked.

"Zyrese, it's not that simple. She is in Haiti, and I can't get to her without losing my life in the process. The nigga that got her owns Haiti, and niggas are willing to risk their lives to protect his. I can't afford for any of my soldiers to die, but don't worry. I got it covered," I assured him, and he walked away with his head down.

"Nah, chin up. You never know. You may have a hand in getting yo' sister," I said and followed him inside the house.

While everybody went to their respective rooms, I went to mine alone. I had four pills left, and I knew I would need them for tomorrow, but I would take two today and the other two in the morning. I couldn't stomach seeing my son in a fucking casket, but I had to be strong in his absence. I didn't want to talk to anyone or be around anyone. I had my own weed and gars to roll my own shit up and smoke, and that's what I planned to do.

After I hung my shit up, I flopped on my bed to roll my blunt. I wanted to be numb until it was time and then to get numb again before the funeral. I heard my door creak open just as I lit the tip of my blunt. I sat up to see who was on the other side, and I knew my high was about to be blown. I looked at Mheysha and rolled my eyes to the ceiling. I hated when she treated me like a fucking child, and she knew it. I got the whole being a mother and concerned parent and shit, but I was good. I wasn't in the mood for one of her lectures, but I was sure she was about to give me one.

I could place the blame on Jahari for this shit with my wife because he shouldn't have been fucking off on his wife, but I didn't. I took it as I shouldn't have brought Zenobia with me, but she was the only one who could keep me levelheaded. I didn't know all that shit was going to tie together the way it did, but here was the fucking storm Miss Jazzie was talking about in the first book, and I was fucking drowning without a life jacket. I didn't know which way to turn. It was bad that I depended on my wife for so much, but she was my rock in the middle of a haystack. I knew she would always be my light at the end of my tunnel and that shit will never change.

Mhyesha walked in the door, then closed and locked it.

"I know you don't wanna talk to nobody, but you gon' talk to me. I know you done popped them pills, and I should call a friend of mine to pump yo' fucking stomach, but I'm not. I just wanna talk," she said, and I sat up to listen because I knew she wouldn't leave without speaking her peace.

CHAPTER THIRTEEN
MHYESHA

Jahari was my youngest son and required a lot of attention, but it was Magnolia who needed it because he'd seen a lot coming up that he shielded Jahari from. I knew he wasn't mentally stable, and that's why I came up here to check on him. I also had a few things that I wanted to tell him because this shit was about to get deeper, and I needed him ready. Just like he had intel, so did I

When Magnolia was growing up, I didn't want this life for him, but he wanted it for himself. I got a thrill out of niggas fearing him and having the power to run the streets. Don't get shit twisted, he could sit at any table, and he wore many hats, but the streets were his home, and I hated that. He had his businesses, both legal and illegal, and he balanced them out well. What I didn't agree with was the fucking pills he was hooked on. I didn't know who gave him his first fentanyl, but it was slowly taking over him.

With everything going on in his life, he was taking more than ever. When Zenobia was home, she cut that shit short.

She even threatened to take his weed if he didn't leave the pills alone. Then, this shit happened, and he was back to the dumb shit. I knew he was hurting, but he showed no emotion and had been that way since his father died. That was the first and last tear that ever graced his face. After that, he became a monster, and I couldn't stop him. All I could do was protect him.

When he met Nobby, she calmed him down a little and showed him that there was more to life than the shit he was doing. Through their hiccups and fuck ups, their shit remained intact, even though her ass was a little rough around the edges, but I understood that. He needed to be smacked around every now and then, and she was the perfect one to keep his ass in line. Now that she was missing in action when he needed her the most, he was crashing, and no one could help him.

I walked over to his bed to sit. Gianni offered to come talk to him, but he didn't know my son like I did, and I didn't need them fucking my house up behind their egos. I knew to approach with care and love.

"Don't roll yo' eyes at me. I didn't come in here to lecture you. I came in here to talk to you because I know it's going to be hard on you. That's your first-born son, and you don't have your wife by your side, but I got you," I told him, and he looked up at me.

His eyes were low and red. His complexion was a deep red, and y'all know how light my son is. He is light bright, so imagine him blushing a little too hard but not really blushing. He just had the red face effect of it. His eyes rolled in slow motion as he tried to focus his eyes on me. I noticed water in the rim of his eyes, but he wouldn't let them fall. He was too mannish to cry in front of me, and I carried his big ass for nine months. He toked the blunt and gave it to me.

I didn't usually smoke after my sons because I knew they ate their wives' pussy, but this would be an exception because I knew what he was going through. I hit the blunt, letting the smoke flow through my nose and mouth while holding some of the smoke before letting it out. I looked at my son and thought about all the shit he had been through and shook my head.

"You gotta give up the pills up, son. You have to," I told him and hit the blunt again.

"When my wife comes home, I'll give them up if they don't take a nigga out first," he said, and I knew he was slipping into depression.

He was starting to not give a fuck about anything anymore, but I wouldn't let that happen. He had fought too many battles to lose this one. This shit was small to a giant. He needed to be strong.

"You know what I loved about raising you, Mahsyn?" I asked.

He looked up at me, giving me an answer without speaking it.

"Your strength. You can fight through anything. I have watched you protect everyone you loved and even kill for the ones you love, but Zenobia is your strength. I know she is not here right now, but you have to be strong for her until she returns," I told him, and he let the tears fall.

I grabbed him by his big ass shoulders and laid his head in my lap. I didn't care how big he was; he would forever be my big baby. He lay on my lap and wept everything that he had been holding in since everything happened at the party. I knew he felt like he was losing control, but he wasn't.

"Why do I feel so weak? I couldn't save her, but I didn't have a choice. It was either her or MJ, and she told me to come home to our son, but I left her. I left her with niggas and bitches that I don't even know, and I can't save her. But she told me to go and save our son, and I couldn't even do that shit right."

I couldn't even answer him because I didn't know what to say to help him. He wasn't drowning, but he couldn't blame himself for everything.

"You can't blame yourself for everything, Mahsyn. Nobby told you to come back home because she knew she could handle herself. You have to have the same faith in her that she has in you. You left, but she ain't too far behind. You know your wife, and you also know what the fuck she's capable of. She good, trust me. Ain't shit gon' happen to her. She is stronger than you give her credit for. You know how she rides for you, and this shit is no different. Yeah, she not here when you need her to be, but it's not by choice because if she could be here with you, you know she would. In this season, you have to do some things alone in order to grow," I told him, but he wasn't trying to hear that shit.

"But I need her," he whined.

"I get that, but God gives his hardest battles to his strongest soldiers, and you will get through this shit like everything else. This time, you will get through it alone. Zenobia is hurting just as much as you are right now because she practically raised MJ, so if she even knows, then you know she's losing it, but she's strong. Let's not forget what happened to her prior to you meeting her. She had a hard ass life, but she persevered. She didn't let anything stop her from doing what she needed to do for the safety of her and her brother, and she lost her mother in the process. Get that shit together before you lose it completely. I can't have that because we got shit to handle in these streets," I told him as I continued to rub his head and the side of his face, wiping his tears away. I knew he was hurting because I was, too, but we had to be strong and come together as a unit.

“I want to blame Jahari so bad, but I can’t,” he whispered.

“You have every right to do so, but you not because of the big brother that you are. It wasn’t Kadafi’s fault either because he didn’t know what the fuck was going on. It’s nobody’s fault, not even yours, because when the choice was made, it was a done deal,” I told him, and he shook his head, agreeing with me.

“Listen, son, I called a few of your father’s old hittas, and they have a location on Zenobia, but I need you to trust me on this. Let me handle this while you handle everything on the home front. They know you, but they won’t see those niggas coming. It would be better that way, but I need you to trust me and fall the fuck back.” I had to use aggression because that was the only way he would understand and listen to the words I was telling him. He tried to lift his head to argue with me, but I pushed it back down.

“Mhyesha, why didn’t you tell me what you had planned?” he asked me, trying to move, but I held his ass in a headlock.

“Because I didn’t want this reaction out of you. We are burying yo’ son tomorrow, and I need you focused on that and this Trahan nigga to put his ass to bed. Let me bring Nobby home. It’s better that way, son, but you gotta trust me.” I had to keep saying that so it could sink into his thick skull.

“You got that, but I need my wife, Ma. It’s bad. I don’t want to take those pills, but that’s the only way to numb myself until she returns. She is my everything,” he told me with so much conviction in his voice that tears fell down my cheeks.

I knew a love like that. Pure, but not perfect. Imperfect but perfect to the people in it. That’s what I felt with Gianni. I knew my son loved his wife, and I would bring her back to him.

But now was not the time. Nobby didn't even know MJ was dead, but she would know when she came home. That was another fucking problem that I didn't need but would handle with care because I knew she would lose her shit.

"This is a lesson for one of you, and you won't know until the time is right," I told him, and then I heard light snores.

He had fallen asleep. The weed mixed with the pills and my rubbing his head put him in a peaceful slumber, and that was my aim. To get him peaceful enough to fall asleep and to sleep until the next day. I grabbed a pillow and placed it where my knee was. He needed rest because it was starting to show.

I slowly lifted myself from the bed, walked to the door, and closed it lightly. As soon as I got in the hallway, Endymion was walking toward me. I nodded my head up and down to him, and he smirked because that was just the beginning of my plan. I continued to the next room where Jahari and Amerika were. I hoped I didn't walk in on them fucking because I would be blind forever from seeing that shit.

I tugged at the knob, and it was unlocked, so I let myself in. Jahari was sitting on the edge of the bed, looking defeated. I guess it was his turn because I knew he felt some type of way about what had happened. I heard the shower running, so I knew Amerika was in there. I walked in, closed the door, and sat next to him. He ran his hand over his head and looked at me.

"What you looking at me like that for? You know I was coming to check on yo' titty baby ass because I knew you were in here crying yo' fucking eyes out or Amerika's tall ass was scratching them out, and I didn't need all that furniture moving shit going on in my house," I told him. His eyes were red, and I didn't smell weed, so I knew he had been crying.

"This shit was my fault for cheating on my fucking wife

with a Haitian. I should have known better than to cheat and with a fucking Haitian." He shook his head.

"Why did you get married, son, if you were not ready to settle down?" I asked him.

"I was ready to settle down, and I love my wife. It was just a business deal gone wrong. I didn't even know she knew where I lived, but she found out. I didn't know she was connected to that nigga in any way, and now look what the fuck happened," he said.

"Well, technically, you didn't kill her. Amerika's ass set the fucking house on fire, but you got away," I told him.

"I sure in the fuck did and would do it again. I don't care if the bitch was black, white, Puerto Rican, or Chinese. I don't regret what the fuck I did because he cheated. He lucky he got the fuck out, or he wouldn't be here either to tell the fucking story." Her ass walked out of the bathroom wrapped in a towel.

I didn't even have a smart remark because she was right. A little of me was in Nobby and Amerika, and that's why I never gave them a hard time. They both loved my sons unconditionally, and I couldn't fault them for that.

"Look, heffa. I didn't come in here to talk to you, but I need y'all to fix what was fucked up and move on. Don't hold no grudges because it happened, and now it's time to move on from it. Everybody makes mistakes, but it's up to you to forgive them. If you gon' forgive them, move past the shit, and don't bring it up no more because that shit is over. I get tired of telling y'all the same fucking thing. Look at Nobby. Wanna be on Bonnie and Clyde shit, and now they separated, and Mahsyn is losing his fucking mind and on pills. I swear y'all stressing me out the older y'all fucking get, and it's getting on my fucking nerves. Fix this shit.

"Jahari, you didn't do anything wrong. The bitch shouldn't have come to y'all house, so she got what she deserved. That's that, and stop blaming yourself for this shit. Zenobia coming home when the time is right. Now, get some sleep because Mahsyn gon' need everybody's strength for tomorrow," I told them and got off the bed and walked out of their room.

I didn't need to go to Janiya and the rest of them because they already knew what was up. I would talk to Khaza crazy ass, but I didn't feel like dealing with his aggressive ass. I didn't know how Yhental put up with that shit, but that's them. I needed to check on my grandbabies before I called it a night.

Mason was already in bed, playing his game, and the twins were asleep. They didn't know shit that was going on, and they didn't need to. All they knew was that they were dressing up pretty and going somewhere. I made sure Cynthia was comfortable in her room because I knew I would need her tomorrow for the kids.

I finally made it to my room and walked in. Gianni was in bed, smoking a blunt, waiting for me to join him.

"Don't finish that blunt without me because I need it more than you know," I told him, taking my clothes off as I walked into our bathroom and ran the shower to take a quick one.

After I got out of the shower, he was still in the same spot, so I didn't bother to put any clothes on. I let my body air dry because the ceiling fan was on full blast. He pulled the covers back for me to climb on top of him, and I did. I needed intimacy tonight, and he felt it. He handed me the blunt, and I hit it a few times before giving it back to him. I wasn't in the mood to smoke anymore because my heart was heavy. I slipped my hand between us and slid his dick inside me. I didn't want sex tonight; I just wanted to feel close to my husband. I felt tears drop from my eyes onto his chest.

"I got you. Don't worry." He kissed my forehead, and more tears came out.

My heart ached for my son because I couldn't bring his son

back. That's the one thing I couldn't fix as his mother, but I would move some shit around to fix his other problems. I hugged Gianni tighter.

"I know you do," I told him, and he kissed my forehead.

I finally drifted off to sleep. I needed this rest because I didn't know what tomorrow would bring.

CHAPTER FOURTEEN
MAGNOLIA

I wasn't ready. I didn't want this shit to be true. This was not my fucking life. This was not how shit was supposed to be. I wasn't supposed to be burying my son. It was supposed to be the other way around. My mother always knew what to do to make a nigga go to sleep, and it worked like a charm. It wasn't the medicine or the weed because I hadn't even finished my blunt. It was the nurturing that she provided for me that was unmatched. She had magic hands, just like Zenobia.

I was the first one to wake up because I knew my mother, and she did everything big. I knew the limos would be at the house at 8:00 to pick us up and take us to the church. Mhyesha handled everything down to the catering for the repast because she knew I wasn't strong enough to do it. I didn't know how I would make it through the funeral, but I said a silent prayer, asking for strength.

I got up, hopped in the shower, and thought about my life and what my mother told me last night. I couldn't place the blame on anybody, not even myself, because that's what was supposed to happen, and it happened for a reason that no one knew. It was a lesson that we would figure out when it was time, and I understood that. I got out of the shower and took care of my hygiene before grabbing my clippers to line myself up. I hit my beard a few times, then went back in my room to put my clothes on.

I hadn't looked in my suit bag because I knew my mother had taste, and she never missed when it came to me. I had to get my shit custom, so I knew she paid a grip. After putting my black Gucci boxers and wife beater on, I opened my suit bag and was impressed. I pulled out a crème and royal blue suit. The jacket and vest were crème, and my Oxford shirt was royal blue. She had gotten me royal blue Ferragamos to match. I had my Cuban link chain and bracelet to compliment my outfit. I sprayed some of my Creed cologne on and walked out the door to meet everybody downstairs.

As I walked down, everybody was wearing the same outfit, and their wives were wearing royal blue dresses. Gucci shades covered my eyes as I walked out the door with everybody behind me.

Mhyesha had gotten six stretch Escalade limos to carry all of us and my security along with us. I made sure my twin 9s were in the holsters on each side, along with my cell phone. I didn't give a fuck about anybody seeing them because this was my city, and they knew how I got down. On top of that, I didn't trust anybody but the people around me.

We pulled up to the church, but there was no parking left. I was glad I had enough sense to add extra security to the team. I knew the city would come out to support me because they fucked with me. The limos pulled up behind the church, so we could go in through the back, and the pastor could pray for us and over us before we went inside. I stepped out of the limo with my four guards, one in the front, back, then on each side of me. Everybody had the same security.

Mhyesha and Gianni were in the limo behind me, so she was the first one I saw. Once everybody was together, I noticed that Endymion and his wife hadn't come yet, and we left together. I didn't think anything of it, so we walked inside the back of Mount Olive Baptist Church. The pastor took the lead in prayer as we held hands and bowed our heads. I looked around at every face because my mind was on go. My gut was telling me that something was wrong, but I couldn't focus on that. Shit would get addressed later.

After the pastor finished the prayer, we headed back outside to the front of the church to be led in. As the double doors opened, I walked in first, and the church was packed to capacity. I knew everybody had questions about my wife but wouldn't dare ask me at a time like this or ever because I wouldn't tell them. I saw a few familiar faces as I walked by. Mhyesha walked beside me, holding my arm, and Gianni was to my right. I looked straight ahead, and the closer I got to the front pew, the more this shit felt like a fucking nightmare.

I walked straight up to the casket where my son lay peacefully in his slumber with the same clothes I had on. His hair was freshly twisted and lined to perfection. He looked to be asleep, but I knew where the fuck I was. I wanted to crash out in front of everybody, but I had to remain strong. I must have been taking too long because Mhyesha tugged at my arm, trying to pull me away. Reluctantly, I walked with her, and we sat on the first pew. My eyes kept looking at my son, and I couldn't shake the thought. I was suffocating. I needed to get the fuck out of there. I pulled at my tie to try and loosen it, but it wasn't working.

"It's okay, Mahsyn, you got this," my mother whispered to me, and I was trying.

I purposely didn't take the medicine because I wanted to be alert through all this, but I was failing miserably. I felt the sweat beads forming on my forehead, and my palms started to sweat. I couldn't sit through this shit. My heart was breaking by the minute. Tears formed in my eyes. I needed to breathe out of this shit because I felt like I was dying on the inside.

"Take a walk with me, Mommy, please." I had turned into a little boy right before her eyes.

She took one look at me, and her blue-covered hand gripped mine as we stood to walk out of the church. As soon as the double doors opened, and the wind hit my face, I was able to breathe. I had security by the doors, so I knew I was good. I reached into my pocket to grab the two pills I had left and threw them into the back of my throat. I needed them to work fast because I was crashing like a dummy and couldn't control it.

"Breathe, Mahsyn," my mother began to rub my back in a soothing motion. I listened to her voice and controlled my breathing pattern until it was back to normal.

"You had a panic attack, son, and it's okay because this is a lot. People came from everywhere on top of everything that is going on. I understand." She continued to rub my back. "You ready to go back in? It ain't gon last too much longer?" she asked.

I wasn't sure if I could sit through it. I was trying to wait until the medicine took effect before I gave her an answer. I took a deep breath, making sure I was okay, and grabbed her hand to go back inside.

Amazing grace, how sweet the sound.
That saved a wretch like me.
I once was lost, but now I'm found.
Was blind, but now I see.
Twas grace that taught my heart to fear.

And grace, my fears relieved.
How precious did that grace appear?
The hour I first believed.

One of the church members sang as we walked back up the aisle. I stopped where the twins and Mason were and kissed them before continuing to my seat. I didn't want them to sit up front, and Cynthia knew to leave with them before they closed the casket. I sat back down, a little calmer than before. I felt Gianni grab my shoulder in a comforting way. I put my head down as the pastor gave my son's eulogy because I was still in disbelief. When he finished giving the eulogy, the choir sang another song as everybody did their last viewing. I watched everybody who walked past his casket with a side-eye. Bitches passed that I used fuck back in the day and couldn't stand a chance to crackheads who came to the church for their last viewing on account of me.

Once everybody finished, all my people stood for the last viewing. Everyone walked to see MJ until it was my turn. I walked up alone because I needed this moment. One last look, talk, and everything before I never saw him again. That shit was killing me, but I stood strong. My hands touched his casket as I looked down at him.

"I got you forever, my guy," I told him. I kissed his forehead, took my Cuban link chain off, and put it in his casket on his chest. He had to take a piece of me with him on his journey.

Mhyesha was behind me, and I didn't know how she would react, so I stayed close. She slid past me and went up to his casket. I watched as she rubbed his hair and fixed his tie like he was still alive.

"This is not my grandson," she said loud as fuck, and I went to her.

"Get off me, Mahsyn. This is not my grandson. They can't take him from me like this." She was crying and screaming at the top of her lungs. Bear came up beside me to help me get her out of the church, but she was strong as fuck.

"Wait! Let me see him one more time. Please, just let me see him one more time. Oh, my God! Y'all let me gooooo!!!" Bear had to pick her up and bring her to one of the pews while the women surrounded her. The undertaker called for all the active pallbearers to come to the front to get their blue gloves. Khaza, Jahari, me, and Gianni stepped to the front as they prepared to close the casket.

"Nooo, don't close it yet. I need to see him again. He can't breathe in there."

I knew my mother was gon' crash out because she was too calm the night before. My mother loved her grandkids, and he was the first one. She practically raised him.

They closed the casket, and we put our gloves on as they told us what handle to grab. The church was pretty much empty except for the nosey motherfuckers who wanted to stay for the show that they just knew was going to happen. Just as we were about to turn with the casket, the double doors opened, and in walked Trahan and some old ass Chinese man who I assumed was his paw, Ming Ming.

I saw Trahan go for his gun, but he wasn't quick enough because Zyrese pulled his two guns and started firing at them. He hit both of them straight in the head, just like I taught him. Their bodies flew back into the wall, and the church turned chaotic. People started to scream and run for cover while my security secured the people who could get out. Them niggas thought they would catch us off guard, but I always was ready, so I didn't have to get ready. Even the pastor and undertaker went behind the pulpit. My people had the place surrounded. Even my mother had stopped crying and pulled out her nine. I looked at my guards, who had blended in with the people.

"Get us the fuck out of here now and take care of whatever damage we have caused in the church. Get these niggas out here and let them swim with the fishes. Make sure all the camera footage is deleted and speak with the pastor about a donation for the church to keep his mouth closed," I barked orders as we walked my son's casket out of the church.

Money made everybody turn the other cheek. Instead of the women walking out mourning, they had their guns raised, waiting for whoever was on the other side of the door. I prayed silently for forgiveness because I didn't want none of that shit to happen in the Lord's house. We placed his casket in the back of the hearse and were escorted to the Westlawn Cemetery for him to be buried.

I knew this shit wasn't over, but Zyrese had gotten the head and tail, so it was only a matter of time before the rest of the body fell. He really came through for me, and his poor little friend was scared shitless.

After I made sure my son was in the ground, and the dirt had covered him up, we went back to the limos to take us back to the house. When we pulled up to the house, it was like a big ass block party. Old school cars lined the block. Music was playing. Everyone had come out to show love. Bad as I wanted to, I couldn't make them leave. People who I hadn't seen in a minute came out to celebrate. Before I even started the festivities, I needed to talk to Zyrese to make sure he was straight. He ain't never caught a body before. I knew the first one was the hardest, and he caught two at one time. I noticed him walking through the crowd of people to get to the house. When he got to me, he stopped and walked away from the crowd for more privacy.

"You good?" I asked him as he looked at me.

"I did what needed to be done. I hadn't seen the nigga at school too much but once, and I didn't like his vibe, but he was bold as fuck to come to the funeral and thought shit would be good," he said without an ounce of fear in him.

"How are you mentally? I know shit could have gone down differently, but you handled business, and I'm proud of you," I told him as I dapped him up, and he smiled.

"My mind is fine, but I have been thinking about what you said about Jadior. I just been keeping a close eye on her until I see her start to move differently, but for now, that's my lil baby," he told me, and I smiled.

Zyrese had come a long way from when he was little and drawing on everything. He still did it, but he was more organized with his shit.

"When is my sister coming home, Magnolia? I need to know before that makes me lose my mind," he asked me. I knew I had to give him an answer that I didn't have myself.

"She is coming home sooner than you think," was all I could give him, and I patted his back as we walked into the house together.

Once we got into the house, all my people were sitting from the kitchen island to the living room, watching us as they smoked. Since nobody would address the elephant in the fucking room, I did.

"Where the fuck is Endymion and Khency? I expected both of my sisters to be at my side." I looked at all of them.

Janiya got up from her seat. She walked toward me and tried to wrap her short arms around my neck but was unsuccessful. I understood she was trying to console me, so I reached down to hug her back. She was the baby of the family and looked more like me than Khency did, and I knew she was affectionate.

"Brother, I don't know what's going on. Nobody ain't gon'

tell me shit because they know Imma tell you. They were in the limo behind us, but then it disappeared." She tried to whisper as low as she could, and I hugged her tighter.

I knew we would be locked in for life because she was honest. That also meant that somebody else knew something. I let her go, and she went to sit on Bear's lap. My eyes read everybody in the room. Nobody's face changed, but Mheysha wasn't in the vicinity, so I went in search of her. She wasn't in the house, so I stepped outside to the smell of BBQ grilling, and loud noise in my ears hit me. Everybody who was somebody was outside celebrating, but I was losing it. The pills still had me feeling good, but I knew the feeling would fade away, and my connect was all the way in Atlanta.

I stood on the top step, scanning for Mhyesha, when I noticed this thick chocolate woman walking through the crowd. She had to be of some importance because everybody moved out of her way as she walked through. I could only see the top half of her body, and she was beautiful. She stuck out like a sore thumb, like she didn't belong in the hood but came out anyway. Her skin looked silky and soft as fuck. Her head turned to look at me, and her eyes were ocean blue. I had to look away because that shit fucked with me. I had never witnessed a beautiful chocolate-covered woman with blue eyes.

Once everybody moved, and I could see her entire body, my mouth watered. I knew I shouldn't have been thinking about that shit because I had just lost my son, but I needed something else to think about, and she was a good distraction. Her fucking body was perfect and natural. She had a perfect set of D-cup breasts, a thick waist, wide hips, and a fat ass to match. Everything was proportioned with precision but wasn't fake because I knew it when I saw it. She wore a royal blue dress that was right above her knee with tan red bottoms. Her bow legs couldn't be missed as she made her way toward me. I wondered why the fuck she had on blue when she wasn't a part of my fucking family. Right before she could get within ten feet of me, Mhyesha cut my view.

"Don't even fucking think about it. You know I don't get down like that. You got a fucking wife." She grabbed my chin, making me look at her. The mysterious woman still held eye contact with me. She blew a kiss at me and licked her lips as she disappeared into the crowd.

"Who the fuck was that?" I looked down at my mother, who looked upset.

"That bitch is poison, and you need to stay away from that bitch before she infects you, and I mean it, Mahsyn. I don't know why the fuck she felt the need to come out here and dress the part when she is not a part of this fucking family. I should kill that bitch, but they got too many witnesses. I'm trying to be cordial with the bitch, but I knew she would come looking for you," she told me.

I was confused as fuck and needed answers. "Hold on, you know her? Who the fuck is she? And where did she come from?" I asked her.

She rolled her eyes at me. I knew I would have to pick teeth for her to tell me.

"The bitch's name is Draya. She was crazy about you growing up, but you never gave her the attention because you were doing your own shit. By the time you came up from the streets a little, Nobby had stepped into the picture, and all bets were off. She had been watching you come up after Mason was killed, but I know her family had something to do with it because niggas knew not to fuck with yo' Daddy, and he didn't have beef with nobody.

"Her family felt like Mason shouldn't have taken over after Hurricane Katrina because he had set up shop somewhere else, but Mason did come back, and business was back to normal. Her father didn't like that, but that nigga dead now too, so it's only her left, and she took over everything. My bet is she's trying to seduce you into working with her, but that bitch is a snake. She may look good, but she ain't good for you because the bitch didn't know how to keep shit on a business level," she explained to me, and I took everything in that she was saying. I was always good for a business venture, but my wife was crazy.

"Don't even think about the shit. You know you got a crazy motherfucker that you call a wife. If you start anything with that bitch, make sure you talk to your wife first because that shit could end in disaster."

I was listening to her, but I wasn't. I didn't want to fuck whoever Draya was, but she was nice to look at. I knew what type of wife I had, and I didn't want to be the next one in a casket because of my dick.

"I'm not. I came outside looking for you and got distracted when I saw her. That was it," I told her honestly.

"She been looking for you. Hence the reason when y'all locked eyes, she started coming this way, but I cut that shit short. I see shit that you think I don't see, and I'll always protect what's mine," she said, pulling my cheek to her and kissing it. "We built our lives brick by brick, and I ain't gon' let pussy make it crumble," she told me and let my head go. "What were you looking for me for?" she asked me.

I looked over her short ass and caught ole girl's eyes again. She winked at me before walking over to her Bentley and jumping in.

"Mahsyn, let that shit go. I'm only going to say it once because the bitch will find you. Don't think the shit gon' stop in New Orleans," she told me, and I directed my eyes back to my mother.

"Where are Endymion and Khency? I didn't see them at the

funeral, and they are not here now. What the fuck is going on?" I asked, becoming frustrated because I felt like everybody knew but me.

"If I tell you, I would have to kill you, and I love you too much. Relax. You just lost your first-born son in a tragic way. Enjoy this because we don't know what the fuck is coming our way, but we always ready." She kissed my cheek again and walked into the house, leaving me even more confused than before. I knew my mother was joking, but that statement held some truth to it.

I didn't rush to get back inside because my mind went back to Draya. I didn't even remember her growing up. Maybe I was too focused on other shit with my father to notice her. That made me wonder about his death more, too. Was it really a beef that caused his demise or jealousy? I wasn't about to relive the shit because the nigga was dead, but I was curious about what info I could get out of this Draya bitch. If it was meant for us to talk, we would meet again, and it would be under different circumstances and motives and, most importantly, without any distractions. I licked my lips as I turned to walk back inside.

Everyone was in their own world. Only immediate family could be inside. Everybody else was outside enjoying the festivities. I sat at the island and poured a shot of Henny to take my mind off everything that was bothering me. I didn't have any more medicine, so I couldn't numb myself, so the next best thing was alcohol.

"How are you holding up with everything, nigga?"

I looked behind me at Bear as he approached me. He was a cool dude. I was mad at how shit had turned out when I made my way to Vegas, but I wasn't because I went there for Janiya only. Other shit just fell out my mouth in the process. He didn't hold the shit against me, and for that, he had my loyalty.

"Yeah, nigga, what's the next move? I know you grieving your son and shit. I respect that, and you can have that, but we gotta get Zenobia back before you lose yo' shit. I know what the shit feels like, nigga. Trahan and his paw gone and ain't coming back, so we need to know what's next." That shit didn't surprise me with him because he was always on go.

"Man, calm down. Janiya must didn't give yo' ass no pussy last night because yo' ass been antsy since we left the church," I told him, laughing because this nigga was crazy.

"Man, this ain't about me, but I need to know this shit so we can go with our move." He left me with that and went back to his wife.

What fucking move? And what the fuck was he talking about? He realized he said too much and was trying to cover his own ass, but it was cool. Whatever they were hiding would soon come to the surface.

CHAPTER FIFTEEN
ENDYMION

I hated that I had to do this shit, but it had to be done. I wanted to be there for my brother, but I knew what needed to be done to get his wife back. Extreme shit had to happen to make sure we got in and out unnoticed, and that was impossible. I hated that I had to use my wife as bait because if something happened to her, the world was going to end. I was waiting for Kadafi to call me with the info Ezekiel had on Khap, so we could make a fucking move.

I had myself, Khency, and about 200 hittas who were willing to risk it all. But I knew my hittas wouldn't miss. I took real good care of them, so they knew how to take care of business. Ezekiel could pull up the precise location and share it with me on my burner phone, so we knew how many guards he had. So far, they were outnumbered by us.

We were in a warehouse, waiting for Kadafi to give us the signal to board the plane. I wanted to let Magnolia in on it, but his mind wasn't right for this shit, and he wouldn't agree with his sister going into the house to distract Khap. There was another part that he didn't know about, which would remain a fucking secret until the time was right. Some shit didn't need to be mentioned. When we were following them to the church, I made sure that we were in the third limo, and we made a detour before anyone noticed. It was just Khency and me.

Kadafi knew what was going on, but I told him to stay because I knew my brothers had my back. Nemesis and Zulu had met us at the warehouse with their wives, so we had the shit under control and would do everything that needed to be done to get Zenobia back.

On the table lay every gun that Khap gave to Magnolia. Rifles, handguns, Glocks, AK-47s, you name it, we had it. We were dressed in all black except for Khency. She had on a pink bodycon dress with heels to throw them off. We made sure it would be daytime when we landed because we had drones in the sky over there. Our time difference was strange as fuck, but it was worth it to get Zenobia back. Black hoodies, jeans, and boots were on everybody. The burner phone rang, and I looked at the screen, knowing who it was.

"What's the word, cowboy?" I asked.

"Cowgirl." That was the code word for go time, and the call disconnected.

"It's time to board the plane," I told everybody, and we grabbed our guns and headed outside toward the waiting trucks.

It felt like days before we landed in Haiti. It was just before dawn, so we only had a limited amount of time to get in and get out. Everything was timed. We got off the jet, and there were army trucks waiting for us. I turned the GPS on and put in the address to make sure we were going in the right direction. I grabbed my other phone to pull up the live camera footage to see what the fuck was going on in his house. I saw Zenobia in her room, reading a book, and another woman, who I assumed to be his wife, in another room, and this nigga was in the kitchen drinking. To the regular eye, it just looked like they were living, but we knew what the fuck it was.

Once we got close enough, I spoke through the radio. “Kill the fucking lights.”

Every light in the house went off. I didn’t know how Ezekiel pulled it off, but that nigga was a genius. When the lights went off, so did the lights for our trucks. I let Khency hop out first and walk up to the security guard to sweet-talk him. She had a necklace on that was connected to everybody's ear, so we could hear everything that was said.

“The fuck are you?” the guard asked.

“I’m whoever you want me to be,” I heard her answer.

I pulled out my binoculars to take a look. I saw her sitting on his lap, and he wrapped his arms around her waist. I knew she would get him because my wife was sexy as fuck. She raised her hand in the air, giving us the signal that it was okay to move in, and we did. The house was big as fuck, but we went to the back to catch them niggas from behind. They wouldn’t know what hit them. We were a fucking army.

Outside of the fucking guns, we had grenades, and my nigga from the military had fucking bombs. We weren’t trying to kill them, but if they put up a fucking fight, then they would lose their lives. All the trucks lined up behind the estate. I made sure everybody was equipped to handle anything that came our way because I knew those Haitian motherfuckers were crazy, and ain’t no telling what type of explosives they had on their bodies. They would kill themselves before they let their king die. I wasn’t trying to lose any of my fucking soldiers. I had four watching my wife. We broke the gate and entered the property. Every gun had a silencer, so they would hear shit inside the house. My snipers were on their way to the roof of the house to take out the soldiers who were up there.

Pew pew pew pew.

That was all I needed to hear as we made our way through the back door. Everybody moved at my command. With a rifle in one hand, I raised the other to tell everybody to separate. We knew what room Zenobia was in, but we had to be strategic when we got her. Everyone pulled down their masks, covering their faces so they would know who the fuck we were. We didn't want to give our identities away, but they knew what the fuck it was. I heard my men behind me taking out the guards surrounding the house as we continued to search for the others. This nigga had people everywhere working for him.

Khap's house had three stories and four wings. He was that nigga out here in Haiti, and it showed, but he wouldn't be for long when we finished doing damage to his shit. For me, it was the principle. It wasn't like my nigga didn't have his money. The nigga was being petty, trying to take his wife and shit, and that didn't fly right with me.

When Mhyesha came to me with the idea to get her back, I was a little iffy about it, but I was willing to do it because I knew if it was the other way around, Magnolia would do it for me. We were family, and I stood on that, ten toes. She sat down, told me the plan, and we went with it. My only stipulation was to let me bring my own army. She agreed but also not to tell Magnolia because he would want to take control of everything, and he couldn't this time around because he wasn't mentally stable.

I went through the side door with Zulu and Nemesis for coverage.

Pew pew pew.

We took four of them off at the same time. We made our way through the kitchen and noticed that the entire maid and cooking staff were working. I pointed to my gun and then to my lips, telling them to be quiet or I would kill them. They turned around, and I continued what the fuck I was doing. The generator must have worked for them because they had light. They were preparing some good-smelling shit. Under different circumstances, I would have stayed for the meal, but I couldn't.

I knew my men were handling business because nobody came to us from outside. Every corner of the house was covered, but my men knew not to kill Khap and his wife because we didn't come for that. We just came to get Zenobia, but I knew we couldn't come to get them peacefully. We moved further into the house, knocking every guard out until we got to the other side of the house, and it was another set of niggas. We laid them down, and I nodded for my nigga to find Zenobia and to be careful.

I pointed to four hittas to follow him and protect him. He really didn't know this side of the life, and I didn't want to introduce him to it, but he had to one day. We parted ways and continued our search. I knew this shit would be hard, but I would leave none of my soldiers behind. We would leave this bitch how we came—together. I promised every man who came into this nigga's country illegally would be back to their families before the sun came back up.

CHAPTER SIXTEEN
KHENCY

I hated to be a part of this shit, but I knew I had to because I wanted Zenobia home. Magnolia was losing his mind without her, and the pill addiction was getting worse. I was grinding on this guard, but I knew that would only last so long before he caught on because his walkie-talkie was loud as fuck. While he was feeling on my body, I reached over and turned the volume down, so his attention could be on me. He just didn't know. Once false move, and I would send him to his maker.

Endymion told me twenty minutes, so I set the timer on my phone, and it would beep when it was time for me to stop. I knew he had eyes on me, but I felt like I needed to prove myself. This was the first time he let me be a part of anything, and I needed to prove to him that I could be his ride or die. This wasn't how I pictured it, but I had to get in where I fit in.

This nigga's hands all over my body had vomit rising in my throat, but I swallowed it back down. No other nigga had touched me like this but my husband. When he tried to pull my dress up, I slid it back down and leaned away from him. I turned to face him, and he was looking at me, full of lust, but he just didn't know he was about to be full of my lead.

"What you doing around here anyway?" He looked at me, and I blushed for emphasis.

I didn't know what the fuck to say because I thought I was caught. I had to think quick on my feet because I knew he had caught on to what the fuck was going on. He sat up in the chair, but I pushed him back down and got close to his face.

"What's wrong, Daddy?" I couldn't even fake the shit because I knew I didn't sound like him.

"Where the fuck did you come from? I'm not gon' ask you again because you didn't come from heaven. You not an angel," he said, and I blushed because he was right.

I had to take his mind off what he was thinking. I grabbed his dick through his pants and barely felt anything, so I knew his dick wasn't big. I began to massage it. He moaned, and I knew I had him.

"I was lost, but I found you."

His eyes got big because he realized I wasn't from fucking Haiti due to my accent. He went for his gun, but I had already taken that when he was in his lust-filled state. Before he could bend, I pulled out my hellcat and blew his shit back. Brain matter splattered all over my face as my timer went off. I didn't have a silencer on my shit, but I knew my husband heard it because of the necklace I had on. Before I could put my gun back in my purse, a truck pulled up behind me with Endymion's people in there. I hopped in, and we pulled off.

I hurriedly climbed to the last row and pulled out my duffle bag. Them niggas knew not to look at me because my husband had them trained well, and they were like family. I had to get this shit off me because I was about to vomit. That was my first kill, and even though I didn't know the man, he was still a fucking human, and I took his life. My mind was fucked up, but

I had to keep reminding myself that I was doing this for a cause, and lives were gonna be lost because of it. I pulled my black all-in-one out, slipped into it, and covered my head with the hoody. I needed my husband right now, but I knew he was handling business, trying to get my sis-in-law back.

"Where the fuck everybody at?" I asked no one in particular. There were four niggas in the truck with me.

"They in that bitch killing everything walking, trying to get to Zenobia, but it's kind of hard because the signal low as fuck, but they know which room she in. We were told to wait until we got a call over the walkie-talkie, and we on go with the truck in front of us." I hadn't even noticed that we had pulled up around the house with the rest of the trucks. After a few minutes of waiting, I heard my husband come through on the walkie-talkie.

"I couldn't find that nigga or his wife, but we on our way out. I got somebody getting Zenobia. Fuck it," he said, and I started jumping up and down in my seat because everyone was able to go back to their families safe.

CHAPTER SEVENTEEN

MHYESHA

I knew that bitch was gon' come sniffing around my son, but she was in for a rude awakening. She knew he was married, and she was a miserable bitch with nobody in her corner. She knew how I felt about her because I didn't hide it. A few months ago, she came to my fucking house asking for Magnolia. Asking how he was doing because she hadn't seen him in years. I politely let that bitch know that he was happily married and he didn't live in the city anymore. I never told her where he lived, but I was sure she would know or find out in due time if she didn't already know.

I told her ass not to show up on my doorstep anymore, but she went on to say that she had wanted my son since they were little, when he was young and wild in the streets, and I told her he was a different and married man with fucking kids. She wasn't trying to hear that shit, so I knew she would be lurking close because she still lived in the city. I had eyes on her, and I knew her every move. She had to be one to watch because I knew she was conniving as fuck, and she would swindle her way into my family in any way she could. I wouldn't allow that shit, and she knew it.

Draya was one of those 'I need a nigga' bitches because she didn't have anybody. She didn't have siblings, and her parents were gunned down in Jamaica when a deal went wrong, from what I was told. That was their Karma for killing my ex-husband. I didn't have any evidence that they were the killers, but I knew her father envied Big Mason.

When she showed up at the repast, I wanted to blow her shit back, but I had too many witnesses, and this was my home, but she was being blatantly disrespectful. I didn't give a fuck if she didn't see Mahsyn's wife with him. She still knew he was fucking married. I hated a thirsty bitch. Always looking for something to fucking drink, but all I had for her was bullets. If she knew Zenobia was his wife, she would move accordingly. She didn't play with bitches behind her husband. I saw that shit firsthand with Dior. I knew she would kill for him without thinking twice.

When Draya knocked on my door years back, she was surprised to see Gianni. She eye fucked him, but I quickly nipped that in the bud because I stomped on necks when it came to him. Then, he had the fucking nerve to answer the door without a shirt, pissing me off even more. I pushed his ass out the fucking way and told her to get the fuck from my house because she had no business here. That's when she went to talking about the shit with my son that I had to shut down.

I thought about the plan I had set in motion with Endymion and his crew, but he hadn't called me yet, and Kadafi hadn't said shit. I took it as no news was good news, so I didn't worry too much about it. My nerves were on edge, and weed didn't make it any better, so I just sipped my wine, waiting for Nobby to walk in the door untouched.

I looked around at everybody, including Magnolia, who

had passed out on the sofa. He was the only one oblivious to what was going on. I didn't need him to fuck this plan up because of him being a hothead. After the repast died down, everybody was just lying around, chilling. The girls and I were at the bar, sipping, but from where I was sitting, I could see all the men.

"What you think is going on right now?" Yhental whispered over my shoulder.

"They probably fucking Haiti up right now, and that's exactly what I want because that nigga could have chosen a different route. He didn't have to be petty and take her. The day he chose to take Nobby was the day he had to know that his days were numbered.

"I should have gone out there, too," Amerika came up to me and said.

"Maybe yo' ass should have because you killed the crazy nigga's sister," I told her without batting a fucking lash.

All this shit was set in motion because she set that fucking fire. I called a spade a fucking spade, and she knew I didn't bite my fucking tongue. She backed away from me and sat her ass at the far side of the bar because she knew I was telling the truth. I didn't fully blame her, but the shit had a domino effect, and she knew it. She needed to take this shit as a lesson to control her fucking anger. I understood that she was mad when she caught them, but there were other ways to go about shit. She could have left Jahari with that bitch, hurting him more than the girl because she didn't know her.

All that shit Jahari was spitting was a fucking lie. He just wanted some new pussy and couldn't come out and say it. I knew when my sons were lying, and I saw straight through his bullshit when the story was told to me. He wanted the pussy, but the woman wanted more. Typical side bitch shit, but she went too fucking far and lost her life behind it. I knew Jahari told the bitch that he was married, so in my eyes, she chose her death when she decided to show up at his home.

I didn't blame Amerika, but I needed her the fuck out of my face, asking questions that I didn't have the fucking answers to. I looked over at Janiya and noticed she had been nursing the same drink for too long.

"Yo' ass must be pregnant again because you ain't saying shit or refilling your glass. What's up with you?"

Every woman in the room looked at the other, but my eyes were on Janiya.

"Nah why you wanna pick on me, and I'm being quiet? Maybe I just don't want to drink." She laughed, causing all of us to laugh.

"Because you been playing with that same glass of wine since we got in this kitchen. Let me find out Bear done knocked yo' young ass up. Y'all be crazy behind them niggas and would do anything for them, but I know pregnancy when I see it. Yo' ass been glowing, but I didn't want to embarrass you," I told her, and she laughed.

"To answer your question, no, I am not pregnant. I already got the twins and Maeyan. That's enough," she said, blushing.

"Okay. We shall see in nine months, or even better at the fucking gender reveal." I raised my glass, and they followed suit. We toasted because I knew her ass was pregnant.

I looked over at Daisy, and my heart hurt for her. I knew she loved MJ, but life happened. She would be okay once everything was over.

"All them niggas crazy," she said, and I agreed.

"That's why I didn't let all of them go. Shit would have been messed up. Endymion was the most calm but deadly of the bunch, and the nigga knew Kadafi. We had to do shit this way. I knew Endymion would stop at nothing to get Nobby, and he ain't gon' be the one to rescue her." She looked at me sideways, and I winked my eye at her. I had all types of tricks up my sleeve that they didn't even know about, but they would eventually see when the shit started to happen.

I knew how to not say shit when it was happening. Gianni knew what was going on, but he knew not to open his pussy lickers and say shit. I would take this pussy from him forever if he told Magnolia. I was tired, though. I was tired of saving my grown ass sons. I had passed the torch a long time ago, but the shit always came back around to me. I could honestly say that this wasn't Magnolia's fault. Usually, everything that came to the family was his fault, but this time, it wasn't on him. This was Jahari, but I didn't want him to start that fucking whining. I should have put his ass on the frontline, but I knew he couldn't handle it because he wasn't really built for that kind of shit. He dabbled a little but not fully, and that's how I needed it to stay.

"You heard anything?" Gianni walked into the kitchen and stood between my legs. He grabbed my hips to calm me down because only he knew I was nervous.

"Not yet," I told him shortly.

"Don't worry, baby, you got the best crew for the job." He kissed my forehead and left the kitchen.

I was confident that I had chosen right, but the shit was taking too long. I knew the timing was bad, but Nobby had missed enough. She was the only one who could control my son, and he needed controlling.

After this shit, I was taking a month-long vacation away from everybody, grandkids included. Gianni and I were going somewhere beautiful to be in peace for a month. We knew the shit never lasted long, but I needed it.

CHAPTER EIGHTEEN
ZYRESE

I couldn't believe I killed two niggas in a fucking church. I used my hands to draw and fight motherfuckers, not kill. When we got back to the house, I went straight to my room with Jadior on my heels. I knew she would have questions that I had to answer. I walked into the room and lay across the bed.

"I didn't want you to see that. I am not a killer. I don't kill people, but my family does, so if you want to run for the hills before you are sucked in deeper, you better leave now."

I didn't want it to sound like we were the fucking mafia, but that's just what it was. I couldn't run from it, but I wasn't about to bring innocent people into it with me, either. I put my head on the pillow and kept telling myself that I knew they were going to hurt my family, so I had to do it. I was cool when I talked to Magnolia, but I was fucked up on the inside. I didn't wanna eat or drink shit because my mind would go back to when I shot Trahan and his father. It had to be because the man looked like an older version of him.

Two to each dome with my twin guns. Blood splatter on

the walls. Their bodies yoking back. I replayed that scene in my head over and over again, praying that it would fade away. I felt a dent in the bed, so I knew Jadior was still there.

"I know you not a killer. Zyrese, you and your family are protectors. I'm not going anywhere. I have seen and know more than you know. This is not new to me. I am just good at masking things."

I turned to sit up, and she had tears running down her face. I wanted to ask her what happened, but Magnolia's words rang in my head, and I chose not to. I looked down, and she had my iPad in her hand. I didn't know she grabbed it on our way out the door.

"Draw me and get those thoughts out of your head. You did what you had to do, and I'm proud of you for protecting not only me but your family as well." She set the iPad on my lap and posed for me to draw her.

I picked up my apple pencil and started drawing. And just like that, all was forgotten.

CHAPTER NINETEEN

ZENOBIA

Something felt off. The lights had gone out, and nobody came to see what the fuck I was doing or if I was trying to escape. I was scared at first but kept reading my book because there was nothing for me to do. Big as this fucking house was, I was surprised that he didn't have a generator, but I saw light coming from the bottom level, so at least his staff had light to cook dinner. I didn't think anything of it, so I busied myself in my room.

I looked out the window and noticed there were trucks lined up in the back of the house. I prayed that no one was trying to kill this nigga and found me. This wasn't how my story was supposed to end. I wasn't ready to meet my maker. I just wanted my husband and my kids. I shook the thoughts from my head and continued to read because that was the only light I had.

The quietness and it being dark was getting the best of me because I didn't know what the fuck was going on. I didn't have a flashlight or a candle to leave the room and find anyone. I didn't hear anything, so I just remained still. I couldn't even get up to use the bathroom because it was pitch black in the room. I didn't want to chance it and fuck myself up because I was clumsy.

As time went by, I got scared because I started to hear footsteps. I didn't want them to hear me because I didn't know what the fuck was going on. When I noticed the red beaming lights, I knew they had rifles, and I was about to piss on myself. This nigga must have had beef with everybody.

I used the light from my Kindle to move toward the window that faced the back of the house. It was going dead, so I knew I wouldn't be able to use it for a long time. I guided myself to the window and then put the Kindle face down on the floor. I sat on the sill with my knees to my chest and my arms under me, rocking back and forth before I heard the window break, and someone grabbed me from behind out the window.

I kicked and screamed, but I was no match for whoever was holding me. They had a black bag covering my eyes and holding my arms. I scratched, trying to get away before I felt myself being thrown into the back of a truck. I was kicking because I just knew they were going to try to rape me. They would have to kill me for sure. It was quiet until they turned me over on my back and yanked the bag off my head.

I opened my eyes, but it was a little blurry. When the face came into view, I couldn't believe who the fuck I was looking at.

"MJ?" I said before everything faded to black.

Sorry, y'all, but MJ didn't die, and you gon' have to wait for part 3 to find out` how and what happened.

ALSO BY MISS. JAZZIE

Magnolia

He Who Findeth A Hood Virgin 3

He Who Findeth A Hood Virgin 2

He Who Findeth A Hood Virgin

Only A Rich Thug Can Fill My Prescription 2

Only A Rich Thug Can Fill My Prescription

A Miami Virgin & A Hood Billionaire 3

A Miami Virgin & A Hood Billionaire 2

A Miami Virgin & A Hood Billionaire

A New Orleans Virgin & A Hood Millionaire 4

A New Orleans Virgin & A Hood Millionaire 3

A New Orleans Virgin & A Hood Millionaire 2

A New Orleans Virgin & A Hood Millionaire

When The Side B*tch Understands The Assignment 2

The Wife Of A Certified Henchman 3

The Wife Of A Certified Henchman 2

When The Side B*tch Understands The Assignment

The Wife Of A Certified Henchman

Magnolia & Dior 2: A Hood Love Story

Magnolia & Dior: A Hood Love Story

Married To The Don Of New Orleans

Married To The Don Of New Orleans 2

Married To The Don Of New Orleans 3

A Nolia Boss Saved Me

A Nolia Boss Saved Me 2

A Nolia Boss Saved Me 3

Made in the USA
Columbia, SC
01 July 2025

60198575R00114